Singing in the Sky

Singing

in the

Sky

S. K. Sigsworth

The characters in this story are entirely fictional, but
inspired by my wonderful childhood companions.

Matador
9 Priory Business Park,
Wistow Road, Kibworth Beauchamp,
Leicestershire. LE8 0RX
Tel: 0116 279 2299
Email: books@troubador.co.uk
Web: www.troubador.co.uk/matador
Twitter: @matadorbooks

ISBN 978 1788039 604

British Library Cataloguing in Publication Data.
A catalogue record for this book is available from the British Library.

Printed and bound by CPI Group (UK) Ltd, Croydon, CR0 4YY
Typeset in 12pt Aldine 401BT by Troubador Publishing Ltd, Leicester, UK

Matador is an imprint of Troubador Publishing Ltd

*All my thanks to the following family and friends
who helped create this story;*

George and Stella Wilcock
Ray Sigsworth
Terry and Toni Sigsworth
Michael and Sandra Miles
*Caitlin Nightingale, Ben Sigsworth, Tommy Miles, Colin
Hollis, Jacky Rawlins, Anne Osborne, Chris Walker, Elaine
Davies, Catherine Eggleton and Brian and Dorothy Daly.*

With kind permission from the following;

Matthew Wilson of Burtons Biscsuits for "Jammie Dodgers".
Barry Sullivan of D.C. Thomson for the "Bunty" magazine.
Justine McKenna of A.G. Barr soft drinks for "Tizer".
Frances Wollen of Hachette for references to Enid Blyton and the Famous Five.
Paul Howard of Sinclairs for "Silvine" notebooks.

First Notes

A white, undecided sky yawns and stretches itself over the south Pennine moors. It lends its colour to glints in the many streams below as they trickle in aimless meanders before finding the slopes that lead to sudden drops down deep, steep-sided valleys. There, brooks become small rivers flowing towards manmade forests of mill chimneys, where giants' mansions of stone straddle their banks. Long terraces of houses surround the factories and climb the lower slopes. All stone from the bones of the hills.

No sign of life at this hour. Doors and windows are firmly shut, keeping out the cold air. Even the clattering of a hundred looms is muted to a dull whine.

★ ★ ★

Primeval screams as two school doors are thrown open to a tumbling rush of children scenting freedom. From the door marked BOYS a small, thin, nimble child chases a football down the slope

1

to the playground. With practised skill he turns and controls it down the lower slope, towards the small garden that brightens the way into the concrete yard. Graham is hearing a wireless commentary in his head, becoming his hero, Bobby Charlton, as "he dribbles the ball past the centre line. He beats a challenge from Smith and manages to keep it in play. Watch out! Here's Clark appearing from nowhere. Charlton sidesteps him and he's still in charge with a chance of a shot. *Yes*! What a goal!"

Graham quickly retrieves the ball from the crushed daffodils in the flower bed, glancing guiltily up at the school windows and hoping no-one is looking out.

"Go on!" Nearby an older boy is coaxing his small brother, one hand held out for the marbles in his pocket. "Please! I'll buy you some more on Sat'day; I'll buy you double."

"Promise? All right, then. How many do you want? I've only got six."

"That'll do. 'Aven't you got any big 'n's? Ne'er mind; just give us 'em. I'll pay you back, honest."

Two boys run by, racing towards a cross on the wall, drawn with a stone.

"Stolen!" they yell at the same time.

"I said it first."

"You did not!"

"He did, Stephen; 'e got 'ere first," says one of the rest of the Hide and Seekers. "Anyroad, I'm on,

remember. You found me first. I'm starting now."
He hides his eyes. "Onetwothreefour…"

Across the dividing wall the girls' yard is equally
active. Five small girls linking arms are walking
along looking for others to join them, and singing
in a chant, "All come here who's playing at skipping;
no boys allowed; no boys allowed."

Around one of the supports of the shelter, race
three girls playing 'Tig Round the Pole', slipping
into the 'den' in the alcove to avoid being caught.

Out at the far end of the playground Amelia is
frog-marching Sandra into the narrow corner. "Into
the dungeon with you," she commands. "Watch out
for the giant tarantulas. Guard the prisoner, men."

Grinning 'men' join hands to make a barrier and
Amelia gallops off. "I must search for more of your
treacherous friends."

Where the yard area is smoothest a group of
children are squatting with pastille tins full of pieces
of chalk, swapping colours and carefully drawing
patterns on wooden tops. Then, with the string or
leather band of the whips wound around the tops,
they are ready to be flung down to the ground where
the effects can be admired as the colours blend in
concentric circles.

"Ooh that's nice, Elaine. Can I copy your
pattern?"

"Where's Flint?" asks Major Adams, alias Carole

Rawstron. The inspiration for this favourite drama is an American cowboy Western beloved by all the children with access to a television set. Galloping over the prairie to join the band of men standing around the campfire in a circle of travellers' covered wagons, scout Flint McCullough, in the guise of Jennifer Wilkinson, pulls hard on his reins and reports that the coast is clear.

"Well, I sure don't like this silence," drawls the major. "I wouldn't be surprised if them varmints aren't out there hiding somewhere. Better make sure we set a watch tonight."

"Reckon it's dark now and we're all having our supper. Sit down!"

"Ooo-woo-wooooo."

"What's that?"

"It's on'y a nowl."

"No it's not, but they don't know."

"Ooo-woo-wooooo. It's an Injun an' 'e's signalling t' other Injuns. They're all creeping up."

"Ooo-woo-woo-woo-wooooo."

"Indians. Run, everybody!" yells Flint, and the men scatter, screaming with glee.

Graham's 1st Verse

Sometimes I hate our Peter. Really truly hate him. Especially when he's mean to me like he was this afternoon.

He wanted to know what were up wi' me when I were a bit quiet like. I told him all about it. This morning in assembly Mr Gastley said he had news for us. It were bad news an' all. He said Fred's going to retire in the Easter holiday to live in a bungalow in Southport. It can't be true. What's going to happen to our football practice on a Wednesday night? Fred's always been t' caretaker here and he's helped all us boys with our football. Every one of us; even our Peter a couple of years ago. It'll never be t' same if he goes. Peter said so too.

As if that weren't bad enough the next thing Gastley said were even worse for me.

"Speaking of our loyal caretaker's help with sport brings me to the next item. You are all fully aware of the rule concerning footballs in the playground. Let me repeat: there are No Footballs to be Kicked Anywhere Near the Garden Area. In other words, you are to use the lower playground only for ball games. Is that clear?

"It seems that yesterday, one boy chose to ignore this rule. That boy deliberately kicked a football into the middle of the flowerbed and crushed several daffodils in doing so. Then, to make matters worse, he retrieved the ball and trampled yet more. That boy has let the rest of you down.

"The culprit will come to my office immediately after assembly with his football. If he does not appear and apologise, I shall ban all boys from football in the playground for two weeks."

Five minutes later I were outside his door. What else could I do? Enough people had seen me. I didn't dare knock on that door. I know what t' punishment is for breaking rules. The strap. Arthur Trickett had it last week for telling a lie and he's still got blisters on his hand.

I were standing there with this awful sick gripe in my stomach and feeling a bit shaky. If I knocked

I'd be closer to that strap but if I didn't I'd be blamed by everyone for a ban on football and nobody would let me forget it. The only thing left was to run away. Where could I go?

"Ah, there you are!" The rotter had come up behind me. He hadn't been in his room at all. Too late now for escape.

"Come in and wait there." He sat down at a desk opposite me and opened a drawer, pulled something out and let me see it. He put it on top of the desk between us. The famous strap, of course. It looked like the instrument of torture that it was… dark, evil and well-worn at the business end. I thought I could see threads of flesh hanging from it.

Gastley took a breath. "You have deliberately disobeyed school rules. I must make an example of you so that the other children will know what happens if they do the same."

Why hadn't I scarpered while there was still time?

"Hold out your left hand." He stood up and moved around the desk. He stared at me.

"I'm sorry. I didn't mean to do it, honestly," I babbled; "I forgot where I was."

"You knew *exactly* where you were. You were out of the area permitted for ball games. Do you admit that?"

"Please, sir, yes. I was thinking about a match and I didn't realise I was near the garden. I am sorry and I'll never do it again."

"No, you won't because I am keeping this football."

He must have heard me gasp.

"However, you have owned up and you did come to apologise. On this occasion it will not be necessary to use the strap. You must learn from this experience. Rules are not made to be broken. Remember that. You may return for your football in a fortnight's time. You are dismissed."

★ ★ ★

Now I know what it must feel like to be a deflated football – all the air and life run out so it's weak and wobbly. Still, I did get out of Gasbag's office pretty lightly. That's what I told our Peter this afternoon and he looked sorry for me.

"Never mind, kiddo. It's only a fortnight," he said.

But a fortnight without a football is a year to me. I asked if I could use his ball now and then. Would you believe it, the rotten thing said "No".

What use are big brothers? Tell me that!

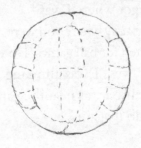

Amelia's 1ˢᵗ Verse

"All right, Pops. Won't be a minute."

My dad always asks me to help sort out all the small items when they are delivered to our music shop and then to put them in the right drawers. You know, strings and plectrums for guitars, strings for violins and cellos, clarinet reeds, and so on. I don't mind because it doesn't take long and I like doing something to help. Best of all, it means my parents don't mind giving me spence!

I probably get more pocket money than anyone I know, except Nicola Potts of course, who always has ten times anything anybody else owns. Poor old Graham never has much. He seemed so fed up today I felt quite sorry for him. He's all right for a boy; nice and friendly when he's not haring around after a football, which he can't do just now, apparently. Although, if I did have a boyfriend, which I never will, it would be someone more like Colin because I could get on well with him. He's an Agatha Christie fan. He's clever and can speak a bit of French. Quite intellectual really, like me.

After school today a few of us were skipping, using my mother's washing line stretched across the street. She was too busy in the shop to notice what we were doing. There was Mousie and her sister, Little Mousie, me, Carole and a girl from round the corner. That's only enough for two people to turn the rope and three to run in. It's better when there's more but we managed some favourites like 'High, Low, Dolly, Pepper', 'In the Garden stands a Lady', 'As I was in the Cellar, drinking Saspirella' and 'Teddy Bear, Teddy Bear'. We were just starting 'Sea Shells, Cockle Shells', when Graham and Colin came over and wanted to join in. They'd been playing marbles outside Graham's and must have got bored with it. Or maybe it was a dare.

Graham had first go and had obviously skipped before. He was pretty good. Then it was Colin's turn. He got all tangled up in the rope and quite red in the face. People couldn't help starting to giggle.

"All right, all right," he grinned. "How about playing something else? Have any of you ever played 'Tracking'?"

None of us had even heard of it. We had to divide into two teams. Little Mousie ran to fetch some chalk and Colin explained the rules. While Team 1 hid their eyes and counted to 200, Team 2 would run off and find somewhere quite distant to hide. At every junction on the way they would chalk a directional arrow on the pavement for Team 1 to follow. When they were close to the hiding place the sign would be a dot in a circle. After the hunt was over it would be the other team's turn to hide.

It's an exciting game and I was glad we'd allowed the boys to play. They do have some good ideas. It led us into new territory too. I'd hardly noticed the gate marked 'Private' up the hill before, but when my team arrived there was a chalked arrow leading directly through it. Of course, we had to obey it or we'd never have been able to pick up the trail; it stands to reason. So I sent Little Mousie first 'cause she can't read much yet, and the rest of us followed. We also bent down a bit when the path went alongside a low fence, just in case.

After a few yards a black cat shot off the wall

ahead into a garden. I could just see a toothless old woman back near her house stooping to pick it up, muttering and stroking it.

"Run, there's a witch!" I yelled, and we all hurtled to the far end of the path.

At the gate we stopped and looked back. Little Mousie looked frightened and asked if I'd really seen a witch. Graham said no, it was only fun, but Big Mousie said that the old lady must have been a witch because she had a black cat, her garden was a wilderness and one of her chimney pots was very crooked. That was a secret sign that proved it. It was all good fun.

Well, that's my job finished now. Only my piano lesson to have when Diana's had hers but first there's just time for the sweet shop while it's still open. I'll be able to buy enough Penny Arrows for the whole week, in every flavour there is!

Chorus – School 1

Eassie Peassie Peckorecka Rare Eye Dominecka
Cheekipecka Lollipopa Om Pom Push
If you do not want to play just take your hook and
go away
With a jolly good slap across your face
Just… Like… THAT!

The teacher sitting playing the piano in the school hall half-closes her eyes, rapturously thumping the keys and swaying in time to 'Glad that I Live am I'. It's obviously a favourite of the children, too, as they are all joining in heartily. It must be the sun's unusual appearance this morning that is responsible for the cheerful faces.

Unfortunately, the headmaster seems unaffected by it, judging by the length of his diatribe ten minutes ago about Doing Your Duty. He had almost sent the staff to sleep as well as the children. Everyone had stoically endured it apart from a few mumblers. A girl had poked Nicola Potts in the back, whispering, "I like your new dress."

"Thank you," Nicola had replied, and then with her irritating smirk, nose in the air, "I got it from Manchister."

More than one child had been pulling fluff from the jumper of the person in front, adding it to a colourful ball kept in a pocket. Mrs Ormerod had ignored it. The poor children had to keep themselves awake somehow.

With the cheerful tune, however, they have all revived; none the worse for wear, and "Well sung!" says the Head, surprisingly. "That will be all. School, dismiss!"

This is the cue for the children to stand, then turn to one side where the leader of each line will lead them in formation to their classrooms. Mrs Ormerod plays stirring march music with gusto until the hall is empty.

In Mr Nuttall's class the children find their seats at the well-worn wooden desks constructed together in pairs.

"English first, everybody. You'll need your handwriting books and your pens. I'd like you to copy this poem from the board and then we will look at it in detail. It will help you when you write your own poem at the end of term."

This is greeted behind desk lids by several horrified exchanged glances. Pale blue wooden pens, some well chewed, are produced and their metal nibs dipped into the ink previously poured by class monitors into white pot inkwells fitted into a recess at the top of each desk.

Mr Nuttall strolls around watching the proceedings, unaware of the silent comparison of pens held up behind him. The idea is to chew further down the pen than anyone else. And there he is, trying to introduce these children to William Wordsworth.

"Oh, really. Is that a blot already, Jennifer? There had better not be any more!"

Mousie sighs and looks for one of the few small patches on her blotting paper that is still pink.

Jenny's 1ˢᵗ Verse

When Julie and I came home from school today we raced straight through the shop. It's the day when the weekly edition of our favourite comic is delivered. I couldn't wait to read what had happened next to the characters in each story. I nearly fell over somebody's dog's lead so Julie ran into the kitchen first. She jumped on to the big chair waving *Bunty*

over her head, yelling in a sing-song voice, "I got it first! I got it first!"

So annoying. I wouldn't care but she can't even read it; just looks at the pictures. *If she goes to the toilet I'll hide it*, I thought.

There didn't seem to be anything to eat, and Mummy was busy with customers who wanted complicated things like fishing tackle. Then she handed me her purse and shopping basket, and asked me to go to Schofield's to fetch a big meat and potato pie for tea. She winked and said I could choose three cream cakes if I liked, to keep us going.

Schofield's is only just up the road. It didn't take long to choose from the cakes in the window. I know everyone's favourite: an éclair for Mummy, a savoy for Julie and a juicy whinberry pie that you can sink your teeth into – that was for me. Poor Daddy would miss the cakes because he works in our other shop and it's his order delivery night so he'd be late home. He'd probably had something nice for lunch, though.

Schofield's smells wonderfully of fresh confectionery as soon as you open the door, with that ding it has. It's always busy and you usually have to queue awhile. Carole came in and stood behind me. We had a chat and she ended up asking me to go for a walk in the woods with her. We decided not to tell our mothers where we were going, just to say we were playing out.

Half an hour later there we were, walking through the park and up onto the wooded hillside. We felt a bit naughty, both of us knowing that we wouldn't have been allowed to wander so far if our parents had known, but that probably made it even more fun.

It was so beautiful. Baby leaves were coming out and some blossom too, in thick white clouds. Nobody there but us. We followed narrow paths, not knowing where they would lead us. Finding a circle of small trees which we thought must be a fairy ring, we sat in the grass for a few minutes. We talked about starting an explorers' club, and all the way home we were thinking about who we would choose to be in it.

Now it's still light and I can't get to sleep. Too busy thinking about what a lovely day it's been. Julie isn't asleep yet either and we've been singing happy songs in our big bed in the tiny bedroom over the shop.

I never expected to enjoy living here. At first it was horrible to move from our real house, set into the hillside of a village a few miles away, where we knew everyone and had a mother to look after us all the time. When we came here we had to get used to living in just a tiny kitchen most days. We do have a bit more space after the shop closes at night and on Sundays, when the bed in our parents' room is converted into a settee, giving us a living room.

The one and only toilet is in the cellar, near the part where the coal is kept, and Mummy has to do the washing down there too. She has to dry it on a long clothes rack hoisted up to the kitchen ceiling, because we have no garden. Coming to live here must have been even harder for her than for us; all this to get used to as well as two children to look after between customers.

I had to change school and I missed my friends. I didn't know any of the children in the new class, and on my first day I had to sit next to a boy, who scowled and moved as far away from me as he could before falling off the edge of his seat. The only boy near my old house used to chase us and put worms down our backs, so this behaviour was only to be expected. My first teacher here was Mrs Ormerod. She thought I was lazy at first but she didn't know how much life had changed for me, how hard it had been to settle into a new home and school, and how lost and lonely I felt.

I did love to look at Mrs Ormerod's special table, though. She kept it full of things that Mother Nature wanted to show us: a real bird's nest; leaves of different shapes and colours; a big white feather with a magnifying glass; and, best of all, a stuffed red squirrel. I had never seen a real one. One winter's day, when it was too snowy for playtime outside and everyone had to read old comics instead, I found a piece of paper and tried to draw that squirrel. Because

I loved it I looked really carefully at all the details and tried to copy the bright shiny eyes, tufty ears and tiny paws with claws on them. I didn't get it finished but Mrs Ormerod looked at it for a long time, and that was when she started being kinder to me.

There must have been a bit of magic in that squirrel because Amelia called for me after school. She was my first friend, and we still get on really well, although I wish she wouldn't keep calling me Mousie. I don't think I'm so quiet anymore. At least it's better than her original names for Julie and me. Because our surname is Wilkinson we were Big Willy and Little Willy!

Next to me, Julie is singing in her sweet, clear voice as the bedroom is getting darker. "My heart is a little garden," she sings. I'm thinking about how lucky I've been to have her through all those difficult months and how we have both come to a much more enjoyable time now. Both of us have good friends and there are loads of interesting things to look forward to. I'll listen and try to keep this memory safe and fresh. I'm looking ahead through all the long years and back again to this unique moment. It feels just as though my heart is singing above me in the sky.

Colin's 1st Verse

No school today! It's Saturday, and my weekly task, to help my grandmother with her shopping, is about to begin. It's good to have a little break from the squabbling of my brothers and sisters, and I'm quite happy to carry the heavy bags. It might even give me some muscles!

We always catch the nine o'clock Ribble bus to

town, and there's Grandma now, dressed in her best coat and matching hat as usual, leaning out from the bus stop queue in her anxiety to spot me.

"'Ello, chicken, I thought you were bound to miss it this morning," she says, passing the empty bags to me as the bus pulls in, brakes squealing in torment. I follow her to a double seat a few rows down. "A thre'penny and a three ha'penny one, please," she says, and the conductor prints out our paper tickets from the machine hanging from his neck.

"How are you, Grandma?" I ask.

"Champion," she replies happily. "Them new pills that nice young doctor give me are just the job." Then she starts on the news updates.

"You see 'er in front?" The lady in question has her back to us of course but I'm sure she can hear us. "Ee, she 'as been poorly. Diarrhoea lasting two weeks. Two weeks! Well, if she will go off to foreign parts, what can you expect? They don't cook their food properly, you know."

"I thought you said she was going to Bognor Regis," I whisper with a smile.

"Aye, foreign parts," mutters Grandma; "eating all sorts o' muck. What have you been doing with yourself then, our Colin?"

"Oh, just school this week. And I'm reading a really good book from the library about a Belgian detective."

"Ooh, you've always got your 'ead in a book, you 'ave. No wonder you're such a good scholar."

She prods the lady in front. "Eva! This is my grandson, Colin. He reads detective books. He's at top o' t' class, you know."

"No, I'm *not!*" She can be quite embarrassing sometimes. "We don't have positions in school. We just get on with it," I explain.

"Well, you'll pass your eleven plus when you take it. That I *do* know. We've never 'ad a grammar-school scholar in our family before."

"That's a long way off yet. It's our stop next, Grandma. There's the cricket field coming up. Hold on to the seats."

I help her off the bus and she walks wide of the blind man sitting on his coat on the grass, his upturned cap ready to collect coins from passers-by.

"I'm not giving him nowt," she says; "he can see well enough to pick his money up."

We take the shortcut to the main shopping street, pausing to speak to the odd acquaintance on the way. Finally, we arrive at the dark-brown, glass-panelled doors of my palace of enchantment. Woolworth's, of course!

"Here you are, young man. Here's your Saturday sixpence," smiles Grandma, retrieving the little silver coin from her purse.

She never forgets to save one for me and it can't

be easy to live on her pension. I try to tell her how grateful I am.

"Nay, lad, you enjoy yourself. Have a good look round and I'll see you after."

Gran takes her handbag and bustles up the street. I know she will do a bit of window shopping before reaching the market. When I re-join her she won't have bought a thing but she'll be able to go straight to each shop or stall that has the best price for every item she needs.

I have my own time now and my own decisions to make. Shall I be tempted by the enticements of the long sweet counter or might it be the colourful wonders of the toys made in Hong Kong? Or, if I walk round for a while weighing up these temptations, will I be strong enough to take the sixpence home to join my small collection in its plastic cylinder under my mattress? I'm saving up for something special but it's taking a long time. As it happens, I'm not seriously tempted by anything today. I must have my world-weary hat on.

Approaching the market, my world-weary hat is blown away by a loud blast of skiffle music; banjo and guitar with harmonised singing on top. It's last year's Number One by Lonnie Donegan, making everyone around subconsciously walk in time with the bouncy beat. From the record stall ahead two young teenage girls, pony tails twitching, skip up to me.

"Hiya, Colin," laughs my older sister, Alison,

beaming through suspiciously long lashes beneath blue eyelids, "Where is she, then?"

They are trying, as usual, to avoid Grandma, and wanting to know which bus we will be taking for the journey home. This plan doesn't always work, and once Grandma spent the whole of the following week muttering about the girls having "no need to doll themselves up with all that muck on their faces".

Of course, her comments changed nothing except to encourage the girls to be more careful with their timing. I think they look lovely. Hours have gone into the making of their full skirts on Dorothy's mother's sewing machine and they've saved up Christmas and birthday money for the pretty peasant blouses.

I'm not the only admirer, though. Here's a youth with a quiff and Teddy Boy clothes, staring after them as they dodge into the next aisle. Hmmmmm!

Whoops, there's Grandma.

"Let's start with the indoor market today," I suggest, leading her away. It doesn't take long to fill the baskets with Lancashire cheese, best butter, thickly sliced local bacon, and the bargains Gran has spotted on the fruit and vegetable stalls.

On the way back to the bus stop, we pause to pick up an LP record that has been on order. The stereogram is Grandma and Great Grandad's pride and joy; their one modern luxury. Like many people here, they have always enjoyed a good variety of music and have built up quite a wide knowledge of the subject.

"Oh yes, here it is, 'Swan Lake'," says the manageress. "A lovely ballet. The music was written by Tchaikovsky."

Grandma grumbles all the way to the bus stop.

"Jumped-up shop girl. Who does she think she is with her airs and graces? I knew her mother and she was no better than she ought to be. I've always known Tchaikovsky wrote the music. What does she think I am? Hignorant?"

Carole's 1st Verse

Sundays are so boring. Especially rainy Sundays. No-one is allowed out to play because it's church and Sunday School only, and according to my parents, if they let us play out, what will the neighbours think? I just know it's too quiet and there's nothing to do.

We took Jimmy to church this morning for the first time. He's only four. He was given a bag of sweets to keep him busy and it seemed to do the trick at first. He just sat in the pew next to me and stared with his big, round eyes. Then, between sweets, he asked in quite a loud voice, "When do we set off?"

Daddy shushed him and we stood up to sing, 'Oh Worship the King'. When we sat down again he said, "Are we setting off now?"

"Be quiet!" hissed Daddy, and put him on his knee so he could see a bit better. After a while, though, Jimmy jiggled about so much that he was put back on the seat.

"How much longer?" he asked loudly. A lady in front turned round and I saw Amelia having a little smile behind her hand. She thinks my brother is cute. Well, I suppose he is, but not when you have to look after him.

Mummy asked me to take him down to the porch and wait for them there. Why does it always have to be me?

I held his sticky hand and tried to pull him into the aisle, wishing I was invisible because now the little monkey didn't want to leave his seat and was struggling and moaning. All eyes were on us, and Nicola Potts, in another new coat, looked horrified.

Then the deepest and most sonorous sounds seemed to break free of the organ to stride in a giant's march along the shuddering aisle towards us.

I scooped him up quickly, struggled the rest of

the way and plonked him, howling, down in the porch. Mrs Potts had scurried after us.

"Oh my goodness," she said; "whatever's the matter, dear?"

Now I'm in trouble, I thought. I expected him to accuse me of pulling him too much. He couldn't say anything at all for a minute or two. Then, between sobs, he said, "I was being a good boy. I waited forever and ever. But the choo-choo didn't start. Then Carole pulled me out and she's made me miss it now!"

What was he talking about? A picture came into my mind of the last time we had sat together in rows. Of course, the little train he'd enjoyed so much in Southport! I had to explain to him that the pews in church didn't take you anywhere and there was no engine in front. You just had to sit still for a while.

"Well, that's daft," he decided, with his best furious crosspatch look on his little face. "I'm not coming here no more."

Jimmy isn't the only one to have had a long, disappointing day. It's been no fun for me either. I wish I could row out to my island like George in the *Famous Five* books. Even lemonade and buns would liven up the dull afternoon. Jimmy is upstairs having a nap, still cross about missing his train ride. Mummy is sorting through a box of old belongings from the attic, trying to find things for the next Bring and Buy sale. Why won't she let me go up there too? I'd love to try on some of her amateur dramatic costumes and twirl around like a grand lady, but she won't let me.

Nothing in that box, by the look of it, although there's something gleaming in that newspaper. It seems to be an ornament of some kind. Oh yes, it's a beautiful golden reindeer!

"Oh please, *please* can I have that?" I'm desperately begging. I know exactly what I'll do with it. No more of this boredom. It's planning time!

Graham's 2nd Verse

Monday morning and I'm eating my cornflakes. First thing, I wa' woken as usual by t' back door slamming as Peter went out. He 'as to get up early because he's a mile or so to walk to his school. Mine's only five minutes away.

Mam and Dad are always first out, though. They both work at t' mill… while there's still work to do there, that is. Mam leaves us cereal and a loaf of sliced bread on t' table next to t' jam jar. Milk's kept in a bowl of water on a shelf at t' top o' t' cellar steps to keep it cool.

It's cowd enough to leave it on t' table today, though. At least till t' day starts to warm up. I'm pretty speedy having a wash in t' washhouse where Dad and his pal plumbed in a basin and a lav not so long since. It's a lot better; we don't have to share wi't' neighbours now.

Weekend were all reight. Sat'day morning I walked down to t' schoolyard. Still no football but I knew Fred would have brought one and some of t' others too. Sad though 'cause that were t' last time we'd have a game together, all us lads from school and our caretaker coach. It were same as any week; first a warm-up, then some training and best and last, a long game. My team lost this time but only just, and that wa' because t' goalie were off form. I got two belting goals! Fred said he'd have a word wi't' scouts from Valley United... see if he can get 'em to come and look at us sometime. They might even take t' best of us on to train if they like us. He's a good sport is Fred. I'm still sickened off about 'im going.

When I got back after that, Dad were 'ome polishing his clogs in t' backyard. Not t' ones he wears for work but his best uns.

"Now then, lad," he smiled, "come and put a shine on these."

I put a bit more black polish on from t' tin and then brushed each heavy clog till I could see t' sky in it. The rest of his kit – black shirt and britches, long white socks and white kilt trimmed with red stripes – had been washed and was hanging on t' line above, so I had to be careful. His hat and sash were on t' wall. Easter Sunday's coming up fast now and he needs to be ready. He's a dancer wi' t' Britannia Coconutters and they've danced every Easter for more than fifty years, apart from during t' war. Dad says it's a pagan custom, whatever that is. They all blacken their faces wi' grease and soot to scare evil spirits away, or it might just be so they can't be recognised. Then they make a heck of a din, dancing and tapping what in th' old days prob'ly used to be coconut halves on their wrists and knees, in time wi' loud music. That's provided by t' local band.

Every week, Dad goes to t'practice. The beer practice, our Mam calls it, 'cause a lot o' that goes on afterwards. I'm not usually still up when he gets back home but if I am, it's a good time to ask him for a favour 'cause for once he doesn't care about us mithering him. He's so merry he'll say "Yes" to owt. I bet he still won't get me a new football, though. It's going to be another long week.

Chorus – School 2

There came a duke a-riding, a-riding, a-riding.
There came a duke a-riding, Asamatasamateasa.
What're you riding here for, here for, here for?
What're you riding here for, Asamatasamateasa?
I'm riding here to marry, to marry, to marry.
I'm riding here to marry, Asamatasamateasa.
Marry one of us, sir, us, sir, us, sir.
Marry one of us, sir, Asamatasamateasa.
You're all as stiff as pokers, pokers.
You're all as stiff as pokers, Asamatasamateasa.
Bend as well as you, sir, you, sir, you, sir.
Bend as well as you, sir, Asamatasamateasa.
You're mucky as a chimney, chimney, chimney.
You're mucky as a chimney, Asamatasamateasa.
Quite as clean as you, sir, you, sir, you, sir.
Quite as clean as you, sir, Asamatasamateasa… etc.

It's Arithmetic, and Mr Nuttall is again rather more enthusiastic than his pupils.

"Let's see, then, if your comic costs fivepence, how much change will you have out of two shillings?"

"Nowt, 'cause if I had two shillings I'd spend t' rest on sweets," whispers someone in the back row.

Only a few hands are raised.

"David?"

"One and sevenpence, sir?"

"Correct. Let's check that on the blackboard." The tall young teacher turns to pick up a piece of white chalk and write a heading of £ s d.

"We start with nothing under the pound sign, two under the shilling sign because we have two shillings, and nothing under the pence sign. Remember, your comic costs fivepence."

He writes a number five under the nought in the pence column and next to it a minus sign.

"Now, we can't take five from nought so we have to take one of the shillings and change it into pence." He crosses out the two neatly and replaces it with a small one. He then crosses out the nought in the pence column and asks, "How many pennies in a shilling, Jean? That's right, twelve. So now we put a small twelve here instead of the nought, and you can see we have another sum. Twelve take away five, Amelia, please. Well done." He draws two parallel lines under the numbers for the answer, with a seven under the five.

"Right, Ian. That's the pennies done, so can you see how many shillings we are left with?" He waits, chalk hovering. Too long, and he turns in exasperation.

"Oh, one."

"Mmmmm. So, the answer is one shilling and sevenpence. Is that clear, everyone? We'll come back to this after playtime. Now, let me hear you all recite the seven times table."

The chant begins, "One seven is seven," and drones on.

Carole leans across the aisle to Jennifer, her eyes watchful in case the teacher looks her way.

"Jenny, are you playing tonight?" she whispers.

"What time?"

"After tea."

"All right. Can I bring Julie?"

"Not really, she's too young. I'm starting a secret society."

Behind them, Nicola is leaning forward, trying to listen. Carole notices and puts her finger on her lips.

"Don't forget!"

"Milk monitors, please," comes the usual morning request, and Graham and Arthur extricate themselves from their desks to push the paper straws through the foil caps of small glass bottles in a crate near the door.

Nicola, still keeping Carole under observation, sees her handing a scrap of paper to Graham. He unfolds it, grins and nods at her. *What can be going on*, she wonders.

Colin's 2nd Verse

It never ceases to amaze me how quickly food can disappear in our house. Take teatime, for example. At first, we were all busy doing different things. Michael and John were sitting chalking noughts and crosses on the doorstep. Marilyn was putting her doll to bed in a box of cut-up material, and Billy was causing havoc as usual, crashing his toy lorry into feet and then into a line of Philip's cars. I was trying to ignore it all, reading my book at the table. That wasn't easy either, having to avoid the crumbs and splats of butter from Alison's vigorous bread buttering.

The sizzling sound from the hob rose, then lessened, as Mum started to slide the frying eggs on to waiting plates. Antennae inside and outside the house twitched.

If you have never experienced mealtimes in the home of a large, hungry family, then you have no idea how strong is the human instinct for survival. Not a single word is needed. Within a split second of food being placed on the table disputes stop and faces appear. Hands weave in from all directions and slices of bread vanish faster than a rabbit in a magician's trick. Reflexes must be honed or a person could starve.

Fortunately, after all her years of experience, our mother always has a second loaf on hand and a couple of pots of jam to deal with the largest of appetites. Drinks of corporation pop (water from the tap) or tea for the older family members wash it all down.

Now that the meal is over and it isn't my turn for the washing up, I'm torn between two choices. Should I continue reading my story to find out whether the last clue to the murderer's identity is yet another red herring, or should I respond to quite an interesting invitation?

A few minutes later the decision is made. Unfortunately, the weather has worsened and I'm dodging raindrops, walking under shops' canopies beneath grey clouds. In my thoughts, I'm back in the world of my book, wondering whether it was on such a gloomy late afternoon as this that the grisly murder was committed. Could the perpetrator have been a seemingly innocent passer-by? Could any of these people passing me now have secret histories of evil deeds as yet undiscovered?

Oh, here's Carole's house, I think. I knew it wasn't far from school, and that looks like Jimmy in the window. There's someone with him so with any luck he won't bother the rest of us. Not the front door, I was told, but down the side path to the back of the house where there's an outbuilding. Three single knocks, I remember. Hurrying footsteps bring Graham to join me just as Carole opens the door.

"Enter," she invites us, theatrically, spoiling the effect somewhat by jumping back to avoid our streaming clothes, "and welcome to the birth of the secret society."

Already seated in the whitewashed interior are Amelia and Jenny.

An upturned wooden packing box and two full sacks are waiting as seats around a makeshift table, and on the table is something covered by a spotted tablecloth.

It's all rather intriguing. I'm glad I made the decision to put my book down for once.

Carole's 2nd Verse

"Now, everyone," I address the meeting. "You've all been invited to this place because you have been selected for membership of a special secret society. It is, of course, vital that no member breathes a word about this to any outsider. Is that clear?"

First of all, I need to make sure that all members will take this seriously, so I look at each in turn. Most solemnly nod, but Colin's mouth is twitching a bit. He covers it up with a hasty cough and I make a mental note.

"Such a society has become necessary because certain things are happening in this neighbourhood that we need to keep an eye on. Many people are not as aware as they should be, so it's up to each of us to be vigilant. Our duties will be to attend meetings regularly and report any changes or suspicious behaviour we may spot."

Graham is looking rather puzzled and I hope

he isn't going to ask me for details, so I hurry on. "Today we must set a password that will only be known to ourselves as members. You'll need it to get into every meeting because in future this door will be locked."

"Are we allowed to write it down so we don't forget it?" asks Jenny.

"Course not," replies Amelia, "or it won't be secret for long, you pudding!"

"It might fall into the hands of spies," I add, thinking of Nicola Potts. "Another of our tasks is to decide on all the aims of our society. I've already mentioned one but we need to think of other ideas too." I clear my throat. "But, first of all, I will unveil our emblem and then we can declare our loyalty and each member will swear allegiance."

"Will what?" someone asks but I ignore them because I want to build up to the moment.

"Now, please join hands around the circle." There is a scraping and scrambling as they stand up with me and take hands.

"This is the beginning." I pull the cloth away with a flourish. "The emblem of The Golden Reindeer Club!"

Colin has another slight coughing fit but I see that the other three are all impressed.

The light gleams on the statuette like an omen as I lift it high in the air. There is an intake of breath.

"Now we must solemnly swear to keep the

society secret and to give our complete loyalty. Each member of the club will place their right hand on the statue and swear. I'll take the lead."

I have to think awhile at this point. I don't know many swear words.

Inspiration as I touch it. "Hell!" I shout.

Amelia is next. "Damnation!" she bellows.

Graham's turn. "Bugger!" he roars.

Jenny isn't happy about the swearing. She is struggling with her conscience but she stands up and puts the wrong hand out. I change it for her.

"Bloody," she whispers, stooping slightly as though expecting to be struck down by a bolt of lightning.

"Your turn," I say to Colin, and he steps up smartly, laying his hand on the reindeer's head.

"Mon dieu!"

"I've never 'eard that 'un afore." Graham mutters.

44

Amelia's 2nd Verse

Drat, I've dropped a stitch! Just poke the needle around a bit, grab a loop, pull the wool through and there, that seems to be all right. This bobble hat is growing very slowly, only a few more rows every week. It's handicrafts, one of my favourite lessons because it's nearly the weekend, and Mrs Barker, who takes all the girls, is relaxed and disinclined to tell us off for gossiping. She sits at the front reading something, probably a magazine or a novel, I wouldn't be surprised. It sometimes takes a while for her to notice a hand in the air from anyone needing help so she's obviously engrossed. Quiet conversation passes the time nicely. She's perfectly happy as long as nobody overdoes it.

Behind me I can hear Nicola, or 'Swanky' Potts, trying to impress someone with descriptions of trophies from her latest Manchester shopping expedition. Spoilt to death by her parents, of course, who are a bit older than ours and treat her like the most precious thing on earth. As a result she seems to have a high opinion of herself but has absolutely nothing in her head apart from the next shopping trip. It doesn't endear her to the rest of us. In fact we're all rather jealous because new clothes arrive on rare occasions and we don't like to be reminded of the fact.

Good job she isn't in our society or it wouldn't be secret very long. I think it has started really well. We each have different responsibilities in it and Carole has thought about what will suit each person best. For instance, Colin is working on finding a code for our messages to each other in case they get intercepted. "No French!" I told him.

Graham will be our chief spy because he is nimble, good at running and hiding, and able to sneak up quietly on enemies. Also, if there's any trouble, his big brother will be able to sort it out.

Carole is our leader, of course, as she had the idea in the first place. She will decide how often we need meetings and when the password needs to be changed. I'm chief information officer, which will suit me down to the ground, and Mousie, or Jenny I should really say, will be our secretary, taking the minutes and writing out the aims and the rules, which we'll all decide by vote first.

My thoughts are interrupted now by a knock, and Fred is here with a question for Mrs Barker.

"The new lightbulbs have been delivered," he

announces. "Would you like me to change that dud one now?"

She would, and all chatter stops as we watch him bring in the stepladder and climb up to one of the huge globes hanging from the ceiling.

"That's much better, thank you, Fred," says our teacher as the caretaker switches all the lights back on. "It's probably the last bulb you'll change in this school, isn't it?"

"Aye, that it is," replies Fred, and with a pang of sadness I realise that he really is leaving. We girls don't see him as much as the boys do but with his cheerful whistle, smile and the odd joke, he's always been around, almost a part of the building itself. Why do good things have to change?

Jenny's 2nd Verse

"Do you think we've done enough?" Julie puts her pair of tweezers down on her skirt. We are sitting in the kitchen behind the shop. A cardboard box on the floor is half-full of tortoises of various sizes climbing onto each other's shells to reach as far as they can up the corners, looking for freedom. Those we have treated are lumbering slowly around exploring the floor, once they have torn off some lettuce leaves and had a drink from two metal bowls on the lino.

When they arrive in this country after their long sea voyage, the poor things are covered in tics. It isn't a nice job we are doing but I know they'll all feel better when they are tic free.

Tina, our Siamese cat, treads between the crawling creatures and jumps up to balance on the edge of the sink, waiting for me to turn the tap on. It's the only way she will drink. She is looking very heavy now but still manages to keep her balance without falling off. It won't be long before her kittens are born. Like us, Amelia can't wait. She loves kittens and says she wishes that her family had a pet shop. She doesn't know anything about the worst side of it, though, which is that it takes so much of your parents' time. I wish that my family was like hers, with time after work to sit down at mealtimes and talk about important things that are happening in the world instead of having to deliver orders or fetch things from the wholesalers or fill the shelves. Most nights, my parents work till seven o'clock, almost my bedtime.

Here's Mummy now, taking a rare moment off between customers and filling strong brown paper bags with poultry food to weigh. It isn't easy for her to find somewhere to tread between all these tortoises.

"Have you really done all these?" she asks. "You *are* good girls. Leave the rest for now. You haven't had your Saturday sixpences yet, have you?"

Freedom and fun at last! We race each other out through the shop, down the two steps and along the emptying street. We are taking our money to the furthest sweet shop today, where they sell exciting Lucky Bags with little toys as well as sweets inside. You never know what you'll find.

"If you tread on a nick, you'll marry a stick," I remind Julie, "and a beetle will come to your wedding!" we both finish.

This always makes us start off slowly, walking with heads down so we can avoid the gaps between the paving flags. We soon get the knack and walk faster and faster, each trying to get in front of the other whilst scrutinising the ground to avoid being caught out. We are nearly running now, grabbing clothes to pull each other back and giggling non-stop as we run still faster. We don't notice the shoes till it's too late. I crash into something soft.

Never have I seen such big shoes and such long legs. I look up higher and higher into a man's face.

"Oh, sorry," I say, realising that suddenly I'm in trouble. He is quite a young man but he isn't smiling, just staring in an odd way.

"I'm very sorry," I apologise again. He still doesn't say anything so I get out of his way and we run on towards the sweet shop.

By the time we get back to our kitchen with the Lucky Bags I've forgotten all about it… almost!

Chorus –School 3

Mrs White had a fright. In the middle of the night.
She saw a ghost. Eating toast.
Halfway up a lamp-post.

As I was in the kitchen. Doing a bit of stitching. In came
a bogeyman and frightened me away. As I was in the
cellar. Drinking Saspirella. In came a bogeyman and
frightened me away.

Another Monday morning and another Assembly. The children are singing 'Praise Him, Praise Him' accompanied, with many flourishes, by Mrs Ormerod. As they come to the end, Mr Gastley draws himself up tall.

"Now, one last thing, boys and girls. As you know, after many years of faithful service, Mr Howarth will be leaving at the end of the week to enjoy a well-earned retirement on the coast. He has given his best years to this school and nobody could have worked harder or more cheerfully than Fred, as we all affectionately know him. As a token of our appreciation I would like to present Fred with a small gift on behalf of us all."

Fred walks over and takes a parcel, while everyone leans forward to watch as he slowly unwraps a beautiful clock for his new mantelpiece. He holds it high, like a trophy.

"Well, thank you, everyone," he begins. "I will remember all of you every time I want to know what time it is. I've had a very happy life here and that's thanks to everyone in this hall and all those who have sat here before you. I will miss you all. Now, think on, be good, and always do your best, boys and girls; teachers too!"

Mr Gastley leads everyone in three cheers and a thunderous round of applause. He continues, "You may not know it, but the job of a school caretaker is a difficult one. It involves, for instance, getting up early on freezing mornings, shovelling coal in great quantities, stoking ancient, temperamental boilers so that you and I don't shiver through the worst of winter days. Not easy in an ageing building like this. That is why we owe such a debt to Fred and why it's been so hard to find a replacement.

"However, I would now like to introduce the person who has agreed to take on all that responsibility. I hope you will all be pleasant, respectful and courteous, and welcome Mr Grimes to our school. Please come and stand here, Mr Grimes."

From somewhere behind the piano a very tall, slim, dark-haired young man looms up and glides over to join the headmaster.

At the sight of him, Jenny gasps. This is the person she bumped into two days ago. Again he isn't smiling. In fact he seems to lack any recognisable expression at all.

"Mr Grimes will be working with Fred all this week, and after the holiday he will be on his own," explains Mr Gastley. "Now, would everyone please wish Mr Grimes a good morning?"

Obediently the children chant together in their sing-song way, "Good morning, Mr Grimes."

"I'm sure everyone will do their very best to welcome you to Thornfield County Junior. Thank you, Mrs Ormerod."

The march begins again, and the children begin their routine journey around the perimeter of the hall to their classrooms. Those recruited to The Golden Reindeer Club have not even the faintest inkling of how, over a few short weeks, their safe, predictable world will become scary, complicated and even dangerous.

Colin's 3rd Verse

For several days now I have been investigating possibilities for an enigmatic code for the new society. My first thought was to pay a visit to the library but that didn't turn out to be much of a starting point. I picked up several volumes in the Crime Fiction section and carried them to a table, where I flicked through them to see whether there were any references to secret messages. My search was fruitless and of course I kept being distracted and intrigued by the random pages I read. A whole hour passed without any result.

To ask the librarian for help might arouse her suspicion of me, I felt. I looked around. Perhaps Ancient Civilisations would hold the key. There was plenty of information about Rome and Greece but I soon realised that we wouldn't have the time to learn old languages and, besides, there'd be no words for "Can't come tonight, it's Mum's bingo", and things like that. We could change a few letters for Greek ones but they would be hard to remember.

At playtime today I asked Graham if he had any ideas. He said his cousins in the West Riding of Yorkshire had the trick of something they called 'pig language' when they didn't want adults to understand what they were talking about. They could speak it rapidly so that it was a complete puzzle to those not in the know. Quite simply, they added the sound 'aig' after every consonant so that, for example, the sentence, "Come out after tea" would become "Caigomaig outaig aftaigeraig Taigea".

Apparently, it's very effective but the drawback is that it takes time to become fluent... more time than we have, probably. Also, I think it works better in speech than in writing, which is what we need for notes. Of course, there is mirror writing but that means we each need to carry a small mirror – not very practical.

Over the weekend I tried using invisible ink. The idea came from Alison's Girl Guide activities, which I remember her attempting last year. You take something like a lolly stick to dip into lemon juice and then write with it. It is supposed to fade completely and will only reappear when the paper is heated near a fire, radiator or in strong sunshine. Sounds good but it didn't work too well when I tried it. Anyway, what good would it be in a dull summer, with no convenient sun and no heating?

I concluded that the simplicity of substituting a number for each letter of the alphabet would make this our best option. We could also have a pre-arranged hiding place for messages at school and perhaps one out on the streets. Anyone else finding a note would just see a strange line of numbers.

Right, that settles it. I wonder if I can scrounge a few pieces of Mum's writing pad so I can work something out?

Graham's 3ʳᵈ Verse

I'm just biting into a butty I've made from t' bread, butter and chips on my plate. All dipped into tomato ketchup. Scrumptious!

"Don't let your fish get cold, Graham," Mam reminds me.

Dad leans back with his cup of tea. "Boss were in this morning. Didn't say owt to anyone. Went in th' office wi' th' overseer. Things aren't looking too good. I reckon there'll be some changes coming."

"Graham, don't rush your food," says Mam. Then to Dad, "It might not be as bad as you think. Remember you said that last year about this time."

"Aye, but trade isn't picking up so fast this year."

I slip the rest of my fish on to Peter's plate and slide off my chair, hoping they won't notice.

"I wa' talking to Jim Ashworth. He thinks… Where are *you* going?"

"Sorry, Dad. Please can I leave the table?"

"Please *may* I leave the table. Where are you off to in such a hurry, anyway?"

"Just out playing. I'll come back afore dark."

"You'd better. Go on, then, but get well wrapped up. It's still cold."

I grab my jacket from t' back of t' door, then I'm in t' yard and sitting astride our back wall, fingers in mouth and whistling to let Colin know I'm out, if he's managed to get away yet.

Well, I've been sitting here a while and he still hasn't come. That's a beggar. He's getting to be a good friend now. Funny 'cause I always used to think he were a bit too clever in some ways. He knows nowt about football, though, but he can't help that. He were born wi' two left feet. He hasn't got an older brother to play with, neither.

It looks like I'm on my own tonight. Still 'aven't got my football back, worse luck, and no more practices in t' schoolyard, ever. I don't think Grimy Grimes'll want to bother with us. He doesn't seem interested in kids.

Good job we've got this new club to look forward to. It's our second meeting tomorrow night. I know; per'aps I can do some spying and have summat to report. I've always fancied being a spy. There's not much going on round here to spy on apart from our Peter and his mates sneaking off for a smoke.

What about going up 'Private' and seeing if I can

find out any more about that old lady, like if she really is a witch? Jenny seems to think she is.

Ten minutes later I'm here, outside this gate. It's very quiet. Everyone must still be having their tea, so they won't notice if I open t' gate slowly so it doesn't squeak. Some lovely big gardens along here but people can still see from their front windows, so I'd better keep my head down and creep a bit.

Ah, this must be t' right house. Looks like nobody's done any work here for years. There's brambles crawling over t' wall. I'll just take a sneaky look. No sign of life, can't even see t' cat, though I probably wouldn't spot it in that jungle anyroad.

Wait a minute, what's that by t' door? It's a broom! It really is a proper broom like in storybooks. Just wait till I report this to t' others!

Carole's 3rd Verse

"Password!" I demand.

"I've forgotten it," shouts Graham from the other side of the door of our HQ.

"Well, you'd better remember it, then. Everyone else did."

"Is it reindeer? Gold? Silver? Anyroad, you know it's me if everyone's there."

"Ohhhhhh! Never mind the password this time, which is Antelope, by the way. Can you remember the secret knock?"

Three slow knocks on the wood, so he is allowed in. A bit of shuffling goes on and then we are ready to begin.

"Welcome, all, to the second meeting of our secret society. Do I trust that no member has breathed a word to another living soul?" They each nod silently.

"Carole?" comes a questioning shout from the direction of the house.

"Hide, it's Mum wanting me to babysit," I

explain, and we all get down on the floor, out of sight of the window. A door slams and after a few seconds we are back in business. I pick up our Golden Reindeer to continue.

"You have each been allocated a task. If you have anything to report, please take our emblem and you may speak."

Three members jump up and almost collide.

"Ladies first," I insist, and invite Jenny to take the statuette. She lifts it carefully and puts it on her knee.

"My task is to write down rules and aims for the club," she begins, "so I'll read out what I've put and we can vote, like you said." She delves into skirt then cardigan pockets before retrieving a slightly creased shiny red Silvine notebook.

"Aims first; number one, we will look for adventures."

"Have you been reading Enid Blyton?" wonders Colin.

"Well, yes," says Jenny, "and it would be a fun thing to do. Shall we vote on it?"

I give permission and the vote is in favour. "Next, please."

"Number two, we will help other people whenever we can."

"Oh, trust a girl to come up with that one," mutters Graham.

"I thought the main idea was to keep a watch

on what goes on around here," Colin reminds us. "You might as well join the Brownies if you want to spend your time helping people."

Conversation then grows a little heated, in danger of becoming a girl/boy split. If we're not careful everything will come apart before it's begun.

"Wait!" I demand, taking the reindeer myself.

"Jenny and Colin are both right in some ways. Helping others makes us good citizens and *should* be on the list, but a little further down. First of all, though, from the beginning we decided that we should be aware of whatever is happening in our own area. Grown-ups just decide things, then get on and do them, and nobody ever tells us or considers asking us what we think first. So it's up to us to notice anything unusual and decide what we can do about it."

"All right, then, what shall I write?" asks Jenny.

"Well, this should really be aim number one," I say, "and make 'looking for adventures' number two. Call number one… erm…"

"Spying," suggests Graham.

"No. Being vigilant," corrects Amelia.

Jenny is busy with the rubber at the end of her pencil. "All right. Number one, we will be… what? Oh, vig-il-ant. Number two, we will look for adventures. Number three, helping people?"

"Well, shall we vote on it?" I ask. "I don't see anything wrong with doing that if the need arises.

Raise hands if you think it should go on the list. Good. So, put 'we will be responsible citizens', please, Jenny. That's probably enough aims for now. Right, Graham, do you have anything to report?"

Graham's turn to stand and he takes the reindeer, enjoying the limelight. "You know last week when we saw an old lady up Private and wondered if she could be a witch?"

"No such thing," says Colin.

"No? Well, what about this? I went past her house last night and there was a real broomstick outside her door. I bet it's still there."

This causes a stir and a flurry of comments.

"Well, that's pretty convincing," I sum up, "but we need more real proof. It's definitely something we can look into. Good work, Graham."

Jenny jumps up and takes the reindeer. "Talking of suspicious people, what do you think of our new caretaker? I bumped into him by mistake on Saturday, when I didn't know who he was. I said sorry but he didn't say anything at all, just stared. I think he's very creepy."

"He certainly is," agrees Amelia. "He's another person we should keep an eye on."

"Plenty of work for spies, then," smiles Graham, happily.

"Take care not to be discovered," I warn them all. "Some of these people could turn out to be dangerous. Now then, Colin. Have you managed to work out a code for us?"

From a biscuit tin balanced on his knee, Colin produces five sharpened pencil stubs and five strips of paper which he passes around. I notice that on each strip he has written the alphabet. Each letter has a number beneath it from 26 under A down consecutively to 1 under Z. We all have to keep these hidden in our desks at school, he says, and it would be a good idea to make another copy to keep in a safe place at home. We'll be able to use them to write and decode messages, which to any outsider finding one will look like collections of bus or steam train engine numbers.

Now he is getting us to decode this:

8,12,6,7,19,11,12,9,7/13,22,22,23,8/2,12,6/7,12,1
2/14,9/20, 9,18,14/22/8

Quite right, Colin. I knew you were the right man for the job.

Amelia's 3rd Verse

Arithmetic again this morning, with a blackboard full of long-division sums. They're all neatly copied into my squared exercise book and I've just finished the last one. Easy!

I lift my desk lid and am rooting around inside for my reading book when Fred appears in the doorway, followed by The Grim Reaper, who is carrying the milk crate.

The crate, with its little white bottles, is put down on the floor, and as Fred places a new box of straws on the ledge above it he catches my eye and gives me a wink. I wonder how long it will take the new chap to become friendly enough to do that, if ever.

"Milk monitors, please," requests Mr Nuttall, so Arthur Trickett and Graham appear and start scratching holes in the aluminium foil bottle tops ready for the paper straws to go through.

"Tea monitors, please."

Jenny looks glad of the chance to leave her work, and we both make our way into the quiet hall, through the girls' cloakroom and down the steps in the corner. It's dark and gloomy here so we find the light switch outside the small kitchen before filling the oversized kettle that weighs a ton. I see to this while Jenny finds a pan to pour milk from three small bottles into, for the teachers who drink coffee.

Next, Jenny begins to wash the dirty cups left in the sink, for me to dry with a white tea towel. It's soaked by the time I've finished and there's nowhere to put it to dry, but through the open door is a toilet, so I carefully spread the towel on the seat.

Fred's here again now but without his shadow this time, thank goodness. "Eigh up, ladies," he greets us. "Have a toffee each and I'll finish off in here."

"Ooh thanks," I say. "We're really going to miss you, you know."

Fred is smiling. "I'll miss all of you too. But Mrs H has her heart set on that bungalow by the sea so it's time to leave. It's a bit small after what we're used to, though. I don't know how we're going to fit a houseful of stuff in there. It's a reight head-scratcher. Van's coming tomorrow an' all."

"Oh dear, have you nowhere to store things?" I sympathise.

"No, it looks like half on it'll have to go to t' tip. Never mind; as long as there's room for Mrs H and me, and our Patch and his basket, we'll be all right," he says.

Above us, there is a sudden gabble of voices and a scraping of chairs.

"Well, goodbye, Fred, and good luck!" we wish him.

"All the best," he replies. "Have a nice holiday. Don't eat too many Easter Eggs!"

"We will," we shout.

Jenny's 3rd Verse

It's always a lovely feeling at the beginning of a holiday. It's as if you'll never have to go to school again. Days and days to do exactly as you like.

Easter time is even more special. At last the first big chocolate egg can be taken out of its box. You can smell it as soon as you unwrap the beautifully decorated foil. The chocolate is about half an inch thick in some places and the egg separates into two oval halves, so I usually break up one half and put the pieces in the other one. It's so-o-o smooth and delicious, yet somehow I can't seem to eat a full half before having to wrap it up and put it back in the cupboard with all the other eggs for later.

That was yesterday, Easter Friday. First thing Saturday morning, it's usually ballet and tap classes for me and Julie but, like the shops, they're closed this weekend. So, for once, all our family can do something together.

We have walked past Schofield's and round the corner to the main road. Down at the glen, groups of people are standing and chatting, huddled in warm coats. No rain, though, luckily. Nobody waits for buses today; in fact, there's no traffic at all. Eyes keep turning left in the direction of Bacup but there's nothing to see yet.

A shrill whistle pierces the conversation, followed by the loud crack of a whip, which makes me almost jump out of my skin. Now we can hear music.

"Here they come!" is the shout, as small children are hoisted on to shoulders. Julie darts behind Daddy. She's spotted the line of men dancing along the road toward us. I must admit they look scary. The Coconutters' first dance of the year comes through here every Easter Saturday, to bring in the spring. They wear strange clothes of black, white and red, and they look like they've come from another place and time. A friend of Daddy's, Walter, is one of the Nutters, and I think Graham said his father is with them too. I can't recognise either of them though because they all have black faces to fool the evil spirits.

Now the band is catching up and they are all stopping in the road, the men forming a square and holding up their red, white and blue garlands. When the dancing starts they move forwards, backwards and between each other with the garlands. I can see Amelia and her older sister playing cornets. They are by far the youngest band members. The old trumpet player looks funny when he puffs his cheeks out.

After a bit of shouting and joking the men are lining up for the next routine. They have circles of wood fastened to their hands, knees and waist so that when they tap them they sound like the coconut shells that the original dancers might have worn a hundred or more years ago. The taps and the clogs clack in time to the music, and sometimes the men put their hands over their ears and jump forwards and backwards. Apart from this it's a little bit like my tap dancing but we never dress up in these sorts of costumes. There's something really ancient and magical about them.

Each dance has its own tune and each ends with the crowd clapping madly. Even Julie has got used to them now and has crept round to the front to watch.

"Time for a pint, lads!" shouts a Nutter, and they're off, dancing back along to the pub.

Home now for more of that Easter Egg!

Chorus – Church

With the organ quietly playing the introduction to 'The Lord's My Shepherd', the congregation settles.

Two young members of the choir, one of whom is Colin, angelic in his white surplice, float down the aisle with silver dishes in their hands, ready to receive the collection. Colin passes his dish along the back pews. Pockets are searched, notes folded and coins chink.

Then, unusually, Colin walks a little way down a pew and something is passed from him to the dish, to be retrieved by a child. Nicola Potts notices this going on and is puzzled. Colin gives Jenny a nudge and she takes a crumpled scrap of paper from the dish and pockets it. Graham, sitting with his family in the pew in front, half turns, grinning at them.

Strange. There is nothing extra in the dish as it is passed along Nicola's row. Could it just have been a screwed-up handkerchief Jenny had dropped and taken back?

Then seconds later there is a scuffle. Carole's little brother, Jimmy, had been sitting with a resigned expression, before suddenly livening in anticipation. As Carole attempts to pass the collecting dish in front of him to her parents, he makes a quick grab for the coins.

"Jimmy!" His mother is scandalised. "Well, *she* did!" he protests, indicating his sister. "She put some money in her pocket."

"I did *not*!" denies Carole, but Nicola thinks she is flushing as red as a beetroot. Guilty?

"Both of you, in the porch *now*!" hisses their mother. "I have never felt so ashamed!"

This is getting to be a habit, thinks Nicola, *but I'm sure something else is going on. What can it be?*

Colin's 4th Verse

I certainly hadn't intended for Carole to get into trouble last Sunday. If only her little brother hadn't been watching as she took my note she would have been all right. At least if she did have to produce the scrap of paper, the numbers wouldn't mean anything to anyone else. She probably had to tell some kind of lie, though.

I only wanted to try out the system, put a little excitement into the long weekend and arrange a meeting today for an expedition I have in mind. I wonder how many members will be able to turn up here on the street?

Oh dear, here comes Carole but she has Jimmy in tow. We'll have to be careful what we say.

"Sorry about Sunday," I tell her.

"'S all right, no harm done," she forgives. "But we might have to find other things to do." She is looking rather apologetically between myself and Jimmy.

"Jimmy!" It's Amelia crossing the road, stooping down to lift up Jimmy and twirl him around. "How many Easter Eggs did you have?"

He beams and begins to chatter incessantly. Meanwhile, from opposite directions, here come Graham and Jenny. Jenny has had to bring her sister along as well.

It's looking as though we'll have to forget the society today, so Carole suggests a game of 'Off Ground Tig' to keep us all warm.

Along the street there are low walls and occasional steps. We race around madly and whoever is 'it' tries to tig anyone they can reach. If the victim has jumped on to a wall, step or anywhere off the ground by the time they are touched, they are safe. If not, they become 'it'.

It's a wild, mad game. The younger children are having a whale of a time and we have to slow down just a little to give them a chance.

After a while we are very hot and in need of a rest. Gathering on Jenny's wall, we sit for a few moments to get our breath back. Jimmy makes an incredibly fast recovery, standing on the wall then showing off, trying all kinds of silly jumps.

"Look at me!" he keeps saying. "Watch this!"

"Ignore him," says Carole, turning away to start a conversation.

Then there's a howl and Jimmy is in a heap on the ground.

"Ow, *ow*, my knee's hurting."

Amelia and Julie rush to assess the damage but I notice that Carole doesn't move. She's probably had enough of looking after little brothers, and I can sympathise with that. I know only too well what it's like.

The volume of yelling goes up a notch. He's caught his knee against the rough surface of the wall and has seen that it's scraped and is seeping blood. The sight of it panics him.

"You poor thing," murmurs Julie, kindly. "Come into the shop and Mummy will clean it for you and put a plaster on it."

He doesn't move. "Come on," she persuades. "When you're feeling better, if you like, I'll show you Tina's kittens. She only had them a few days ago and they've still got their eyes shut. No-one but us has seen them yet. You'll have to be very quiet."

The howls quickly subside to the hiccup stage as we consider whether young Julie might be a genius. I realise that this may be the opportunity we need.

"Julie, would you do something for us, please? We have to go on an errand for a while. It'll take about half an hour. Can you look after Jimmy till we come back?"

Fortunately she nods as Jimmy takes her hand, putting on a bit of a stagger as they disappear round the corner.

"Now, we'll have to be really quick," I warn

the others. "Remember how one of our Golden Reindeer aims is to have adventures? Well, how about this one? Not far from the library is the old house that used to belong to the doctor, where he had the surgery in one of the rooms. You most likely went to it? Right, well, nobody's lived there for years. It's going to be demolished for a new bus turn-round. I took a look at it yesterday and the door was unlocked. Would anyone like to explore?"

"You bet!" grins Graham, eyes shining.

"It's probably full of ghosts and ghoulies," gloats Amelia, relishing the idea.

"Better still," beams Graham. "Let's go!"

★ ★ ★

It's a jungle around the old house, rather like the witch's garden but even worse. After racing along the road then down what's still just about a pathway under encroaching branches that seem to be snatching at our clothes, we find the wrought-iron gate that now hangs permanently open.

We are all slowing down, so that in front of the worn wooden door we come to a dead stop. This door, which from my position at the gate had looked slightly ajar yesterday, now appears to be firmly closed.

"It's almost as if it's telling us to keep out," mutters Jenny, echoing my thoughts. The varnish on the surface has peeled and curled, uncared for, unloved. Maybe someone has locked the house up again.

"Go on, then!" Graham encourages, so I grasp the large handle, twist it and, surprisingly, the door swings back.

An unwelcoming odour of damp plaster greets us, followed by overtones of decay. Darkness almost hides the cause of the smell but I can vaguely make out piles of rubble against inner doorways to either side of a wide hall that stretches back into obscurity. At the top of the staircase before us the darkness is relieved slightly, albeit with a hazy light which is strange and yellowish, making my vision seem indistinct and uncertain. There is no sound at all.

"It feels as if something's waiting for us." Although Carole whispers, her voice sounds too loud. We share a collective mental shiver.

"Perhaps we shouldn't go right in, after all," I decide. "It looks quite dangerous."

We back out and turn, only to notice the rain. On the way, it was spotting slightly but now it is becoming a downpour. None of us has a raincoat so reluctantly we step back into the hallway to shelter.

"Perhaps we boys should come back on our own in the morning," I suggest.

Amelia immediately turns on me. "Oh no you don't," she objects. "Come on girls!" and, would you believe it, the three of them are suddenly ahead of Graham and I, climbing the wide staircase in front of us. When I say 'climbing', after the first few steps it becomes more of an extremely hesitant ascent. We bunch together in silence again, noticing the sharp cracks and complaints of each stair tread whilst trying to see through the gathering gloom up to the landing above.

Even I think I can sense that we are being observed, and the feeling is increasingly insistent. Although there is still a background of silence, there are small, indistinct noises below. Could the house be waking up, wishing us harm?

I don't know if any of us makes a small movement but it's suddenly as if we all turn as one. Clattering rapidly downstairs, we lurch towards the door.

"Wait!" Graham finds his voice. "Did you notice that?" He is hanging on to the open door, pointing backwards into the hall.

"What?" I ask.

"Just look there, further along t' floor!"

We look. A line of large wet footprints lead down as far as we can see. One of us screams, we all race out, along the path, oblivious of the rain, and back to the world of safety, and little Jimmy.

Carole's 4th Verse

It's not fair. I've just been round to the music shop to collect Amelia. Her dad said she wasn't in and had gone round to Jenny's to see their new Siamese kittens.

She's always playing with Jenny now and she used to be *my* best friend. I haven't got a best friend anymore. At least I've got The Golden Reindeer Club. It's had a really good start but I'll need to think of some more adventures and other things to keep it interesting.

I wasn't very happy about Colin deciding what we were going to do last week and giving out secret messages to arrange a meeting. That's the trouble with boys. Once you let them into something they want to take control.

I'm so fed up, I've even got round to scrubbing the wooden plasticine boards we all have to take home from school at holiday times. The younger children roll snakes and make them into letters to help them learn, and we all use plasticine sometimes when it's too cold to play out. If it's just wet we are out under the shelter.

It's all right for the teachers, nice and warm and dry inside with their cups of tea. They never come out, just throw the odd glance through the window to check we aren't murdering each other.

I loved it one wet day recently when someone had the idea of jiving. I don't know who started it but it wasn't long before nearly all the girls were yelling, "One, two, three o'clock, four o'clock, rock!" pulling our partners in and out and twirling around. We soon warmed up that time. No boys around and we had loads of fun.

I suppose I have to admit that it was a good idea of Colin's to go exploring that old house. It was a bit frightening, though, especially when we saw those footprints. To think that somebody must have walked in while we were actually there!

It wouldn't surprise me if it turned out to be that new caretaker. He's creepy enough to do that kind of thing and he has big enough feet too.

I need to think up some more adventures like that or discover some mysteries to solve before the boys do it all. I'm not going back there again on my own but maybe I could take a look at the witch's house, see if she's up to anything. I might call for Graham. He's good at sneaking and, after all, he is our spy. I'll just get my coat and try his house while these boards drain.

Graham's 4th Verse

Well this is summat I've never done afore. We're sitting on t' grass wi' fishing rods, just me and my pal, Michael. There's loads of other kids in different spots around this mill lodge up in t' hills.

It's like a different country here. Just sky, water and grass. No cobbled streets or mill chimneys except for one tumbledown one where an old mill used to be. Music too, provided by birdsong. Skylarks, Michael says, are the singers in the sky.

He seems to know a lot of things, does Michael. He's lent me his rod and he's using his dad's, though I don't think his dad knows owt about it.

Michael showed me how to bait the hook. He had a tin in his pocket and when he opened it, it were full of wriggling worms and maggots. A bit of a surprise to me, and I must have jumped because it made Michael laugh. He told me not to worry, we weren't going to keep t' maggots warm to wake 'em up like some fishermen do, putting 'em in our mouths. They were lively enough already, and a good job too.

The lines have floats attached to 'em so you can see where they are when you've looped 'em up and hurled 'em as far as you can into t' water. A split lead shot keeps th' hook end o' t' line weighted down.

We've been sat like this some time now. We did have a break when I got t' sandwiches out. They were tomatoes on sliced white bread, squashy in greaseproof paper and good; just right for two hungry fisherboys. I've got my mam to thank for them.

I haven't caught owt yet but an hour or so ago Michael's line twitched. It were reight exciting. You could see summat in t' water jumping about. Then really carefully he managed to land a fish about t' size of his hand. A perch, he said it were, and too small to take home.

He let me look at it so I could see it breathing through its gills. I wanted to look longer but he said it'd die if I weren't quick. When I let it go it didn't move and I thought it were my fault. Then it gave a wriggle and swam away like a rocket.

Since then, no more bites. One or two o' t' other lads have been lucky. They don't half shout when they get something. Lucky for us, Michael said, because all t' fish'd swim over to our side.

No chance of that now. A group of scruffy young kids, who've no idea what they're doing, arrived five minutes ago. They're making a heck of a racket, messing about with old planks of wood. I nearly shouted at 'em to get out of our way but at least it's got entertainment value, watching, after we've been sitting so long.

They're throwing t' planks in t' water longways, sideways, all ways and dive bombing 'em wi' clods of earth, trying to race their own with each other's. Planks are going nowhere 'cause there's no current. It's a comedy act.

Now there's a great splash and commotion. One of 'em seems to have thrown himself in as well, silly devil.

Wait a minute, he's thrashing about. His pals are going frantic.

"Tom, get *out*!" One of them's trying to hold a plank out to him but it won't reach, he's too far away. It's pandemonium.

"He can't swim; *help*!" yells another lad to everyone around the shore.

Michael and I are nearest but we can't swim either; school doesn't take us till next year. All t' other kids are on their feet, not moving, hypnotised. There's no adults around.

Adults! I nearly fly over t' grass to the footpath, pelt along it to the lane, down towards t' first row of houses. It'll be no use, though; no-one'll be at home; they'll all be at work at this time.

There's the gable end and little gardens in front, empty. No, someone's there, straightening up with a trowel in his hand.

I can hardly speak, I'm so out of breath. Don't know what I gabble but the man catches on fast. I can't keep pace as he races up to the lodge.

I see him ahead, not stopping by t' water's edge, plunging straight in. As I get there, still gasping, he's bringing t' lad out. The boy is limp in his arms. It must be too late. He's laid him down on t' grass.

If only I'd gone a few seconds sooner. If only I'd run faster. This is horrible, horrible.

I can't look at him anymore. I'm staring at our

rods, my jacket and the greaseproof paper from our sandwiches.

I know t' man is still wi' t' boy. There's absolute silence now. All t' other kids are stunned. It could be any of us on t' grass. I don't want to be 'ere anymore. This can't be 'appening. Not to me. Not to that little lad so still over there.

The man has rolled him over. He's sat him up and thumped his back and now he's working on his chest. I wish he'd stop. Can't he see t' poor thing has had it?

But now there's a cough and a splutter. Not the man, the boy. He's coming back to life!

We just gawp; can't do owt else. Can't believe what's just happened. The man, soaking wet, looks round at us.

"He's all right now, lads. But he might need a doctor. Can somebody go and ring 999?"

An older couple of friends who've come closer set off down t' path to find a telephone box. I'm glad it's not up to me this time 'cause I'm feeling shaky and have to sit down. Michael sits with me, and the others have come to stand around. We don't go anywhere, any of us. After a while an ambulance crew arrives to take over, soon followed by two policemen. They ask a lot of questions.

All this time, I'm thinking, well, we were looking for adventures in The Golden Reindeer Club. But I never want another one like this. Ever!

Amelia's 4th Verse

Jenny and Julie have no idea how lucky they are. Our fathers are in the same line of work, both shopkeepers. They are both successful, both members of the Board of Trade. But there the similarities end. There isn't really much that interests me in our business. It's all quite predictable, whereas for Jenny there's always something new.

They have a bushbaby from Africa now, in their other, larger shop. It was at home with them over the weekend, and I saw it today, fast asleep, curled in a furry ball. Apparently it wakes up at night and watches TV with huge round eyes as big as saucers.

Sometimes they have the monkey at home. It's full of tricks and will reach through the bars of its cage to tear off strips of wallpaper. They take it for walks using a tiny harness with a long lead. Last time, it climbed to the top of a bus-stop sign so fast that it pulled the lead right out of Jenny's hand.

Luckily she managed to grab it again while Sinbad was sitting watching the world go by.

This morning I went round to see the kittens. Their eyes are open now so they are getting more inquisitive and moving around, pawing and tumbling over each other. They are still a bit unsteady on their feet. They have blue eyes, little black ears and noses, and are completely adorable. So soft to touch, too.

The three of us made toys for them, threading pieces of wool through foil bottle tops so we could dangle them in the air or pull them along the lino. The kittens couldn't leave them alone. Their heads turned to follow every move as they pawed, pounced and bounced, sometimes losing balance and rolling over.

All too soon Mrs Wilkinson asked us to put the kittens back in their box bed. Tina was prowling anxiously, wanting to feed them. We watched a while, wondering what to do next.

"*I* know," I offered. "Why don't you come across to the workshop and have a look at our Old Humbers?"

I took both Big *and* Little Mousie because Julie's sweet and I didn't want to leave her on her own. The workshop would be unlocked as it always is, leaking its perfume of engine oil, worn leather seats and mildewed sheets that Pops uses to cover the two ancient cars.

I knew he wouldn't really mind; it wasn't as if I was taking hoodlums in there to wreck the place. But I wanted to make it mysterious, so I opened the door painfully slowly and peered round it to "see if the coast was clear". I left the switch off to let the dim light add to the effect. Goodness knows what this old building used to be but now it's only used for my father and uncle's shared passion: the renovation of classic cars.

First there's a small whitewashed room lined with dipping shelves full of spare parts, metal tools, oil cans and yellowing car catalogues. We tiptoed through here towards the 'inner sanctum'. I made a show of listening in case my uncle was at work. Silence, so we crept through to examine the cars, which sit side by side, waiting to be coaxed and cajoled piece by rusty piece back to life.

One of them, the oldest, looks so decrepit and

forlorn that it must only be useful for its engine parts. The other has a bonnet that gleams with care and attention.

We had to squeeze between them to get to the far end of the workshop. "This place has seen better days. Watch this!" I told them, finding a hole in the whitewashed wall and poking a finger into it. Wriggling around a bit loosens the deteriorating surface so I soon had a trickle of white powder flowing down the wall and onto the floor.

"Find a hole, both of you," I invited, and after a quick look round they did. Before long we all had a satisfying pile of powder, each in serious competition to gather the most.

It struck me then that Pops and Uncle Raymond would realise that these growing heaps were not due to natural causes. Whoops, time to stop.

"Come and sit in the darkest corner," I persuaded, and when they had settled in it I sang them the spooky song my sister had taught me about a ghost with her head tucked underneath her arm.

I could see they were enthralled. It's a wonderfully chilling song. I sang it in a low, slow voice, crawling my fingers up Julie's spine at one point in the song. I hope she doesn't have nightmares tonight!

Jenny's 4th Verse

School again, and we're all in the cloakroom taking off soggy hats and coats, hanging them up and changing out of muddy shoes into our pumps.

It's nice to see everyone again and share a quick chat about holiday news. Nicola Potts is listening, of course, and showing off her new raincoat. It's a beautiful powder-blue colour that matches her eyes, and we're so jealous. How can such an everyday thing as a raincoat be so gorgeous? Trust *her* to have found one. All eyes follow her as she sweeps out, and I realise I've had enough of her.

Before I can think what I'm doing, I grab an empty wastepaper basket, jam it down on my head and jump onto the nearest cloakroom bench. I saunter up and down it with my chin in the air. How does it feel to be Nicola?

"D'you like my new hat?" I simper, fluttering my eyelashes. "I got it from Manchister."

I love it when everybody laughs so I put on even more of a smirk and try out a shoulder wriggle. "It's the latest fashion."

There's some delighted chuckling, and I'm trying to think of what else I can add to it when, heaven forbid! There's Nicola herself standing at the door to the hall, watching.

I feel so guilty. I do hope she hasn't heard anything.

But she obviously has. She quickly turns and goes away, looking at the ground.

"Exit, stage right!" breathes Carole.

Colin's 5th Verse

For once it was an interesting Assembly this morning. It was Mrs Barker's turn because Mr Gastley had an inspector with him. Apparently we could be expecting a class visit this afternoon.

Mrs Barker began by asking us to remember the last time we had played 'Blind Man's Buff' at a party. We had to envisage wearing a thick, well-tied blindfold. Then we had to take it a stage further and imagine cotton wool in our ears as well.

"Think how difficult it would be to find anybody," she said. "Even to find your way around the room. No sight and no sound to guide you, only touch."

This was rather a good introduction, making each one of us receptive to her account of the life of Helen Keller. It was inspirational to learn how Helen had overcome the effects of such an unlucky event in her early childhood, which had robbed her of sight and hearing. She had been resourceful enough in her silent loneliness to learn how to use the Braille system, which she later made known worldwide so that life would be easier for all blind people in the future.

Unfortunately, it also had a more negative effect on me. It reminded me of the fact that, for two years now, I have needed spectacles. It's probably the result of my insatiable reading habits and dim lighting but it's rather worrying when I need a stronger prescription after each eye test. The rest of my family seem unaffected. I'm quite used to wearing glasses and wouldn't want to be without them now, really. People say they make me look intelligent, which is nice, but I do hope my sight will stabilise.

I was deep in thought about this while Mrs Ormerod was playing the usual marching tune with her customary flourishes. Last in line, walking towards the classroom, an unexpected tap on my shoulder startled me.

Behind me, the new caretaker had appeared without a sound. He said nothing, simply handing me an envelope with Mr Nuttall's name on it, before leaving as silently as he had come.

The others are right. There certainly is something quite strange about him. A most suspicious character indeed.

Carole's 5th Verse

School was a bit different today. In the hall this morning we had an interesting talk about Helen Keller and how she took control of her life despite having so much to overcome. It just shows what we can all do when we are determined.

In class, Colin gave Mr Nuttall a message in an envelope. For a moment I was horrified, thinking he was inviting him to our next meeting!

Mr N didn't look too happy as he was reading it and he screwed it up and threw it in the bin. Another mystery!

We had Arithmetic again. We were told we'd got rusty after the holiday and we needed to pull our socks up. Mr Nuttall kept glancing at the door, rather anxiously it seemed. We drank milk as usual before playtime but he didn't ask the monitors to make the teachers' drinks.

It was a wet playtime and the rain must have been extra hard because we had to stay indoors.

Mr N wasn't happy about that either. He found a stack of paper for us to draw on and stayed with us, strangely enough, marking a pile of books.

We were allowed to talk quietly but Nicola was still very troubled, not speaking to anyone. I felt quite sorry for her actually, even though she is such a pain. I know how it feels to think you've no friends so I gave her one of my Jammie Dodgers.

This afternoon, last lesson, we were each given a book with a play in it, written out in different parts.

I was the Lady of the Manor and had to tell the servants what to do. I put on my best bossy voice and was enjoying it, when a stranger came in. He sat down at the back of the class and we were asked to continue.

I rather enjoyed showing off to him and I could tell that Amelia was doing the same. She had the role of the parlourmaid and was speaking in a cheeky voice. Colin was the Chief Inspector, well cast. It was funny how all the best readers had the parts... no hesitant ones. For once we were all sorry when we had to stop for home time. Why can't we do this every day?

Graham's 5th Verse

I've got my football back! Gasbags brought it round to our classroom this morning just before playtime and handed it over. With a few wise words, of course; he can never resist that.

It were like seeing an old friend again after years apart. Just having it in my hands, turning it round, made me feel so much better. I've missed it every day, especially in t' holidays. Peter did let me have a kick-about with his in the end, but it weren't same.

I've more or less recovered after that scare up at t' fishing lodge. So glad it worked out all right. Mam and Dad had a surprise a couple o' nights later when someone knocked on t' door and said she were a reporter from t' *Free Press*. Could she have a word wi' me?

You should have seen their faces! They thought I must have got into mischief. She came in an' sat at t' table wi' her notepad. She made me remember every detail. Said it'd be in t' paper later this week. She had a camera and took a picture of me too.

Mam and Dad could hardly believe it when they heard t' story. I'd never said nowt. It weren't me that saved him.

Anyroad, I've got my football now and I'm *carrying* it down t' slope this time. Well away from t' flower bed, just to be certain!

Now I can kick it.

What the heck? That daft little squirt from 1B who's always following me around has got it. Where's he taking it? Not back to the garden, please!

Look at that! He's given it a reight punce. It's banged on t' boiler room door under t' classrooms. Door can't have been locked 'cause t' ball's pushed it open and gone right through. And the silly beggar's run off.

I'm not bound to lose my football when I've only just got it back. I sidle up to t' wall in case there's any teachers looking out. Once there, they shouldn't be able to see me directly underneath. Now all it'll take will be a quick dash.

Urrrrrgh! There's a horrible stench coming from somewhere in here. It's sickening! There's my ball in front of loads of old sacks stacked up. Probably prize manure for t' garden. I'll grab my ball quick before t' stink gets to it. Now, slam t' door shut so nobody knows it's been open.

That were close. Just as I slammed it I saw a tall

dark shape moving towards me. Must have been that creepy caretaker. Good job no lights were on; I don't think he'd know who I was.

Amelia's 5ᵗʰ Verse

I called for Carole after tea today. We couldn't think of anything to do till she remembered something. She said she'd been wanting to keep an eye on the witch because Graham seemed to have forgotten. She hadn't wanted to go on her own, so now would be a good chance.

First, she fetched a little booklet she'd hidden in the clubhouse. She'd had it since last year, when her family had been for an outing to Pendle Hill. There was a special shop in one of the villages there, full of souvenirs about the Lancashire Witches, who lived in that area and were tried and hanged in Lancaster in the seventeenth century.

Jimmy had been given a little witch on a broomstick to take home and hang in his window, and Carole had asked for the booklet. She'd only read bits of it so now we decided to have a quick look before going on our witch hunt.

I flicked through the pages till a heading caught my eye.

FAMILIARS

The animal reputed to be most frequently associated with a witch is a black cat, although occasional use of a toad or crow is mentioned.

Right, we'll watch out for them as well. The next page was interesting too.

HERBAL LORE

Potions can be made from a wealth of herbs, some of which may be used for good and some for ill. Herbs used for poisoning include Deadly Nightshade...

We thrilled at the sound of Deadly Nightshade, and stared, fascinated, at the drawing of the plant on the page.

"I know," I suggested. "Let's go and see if there's any of this in the witch's garden. If there is, it will be the proof we need, and we'll be able to tell the others at the next meeting."

I could tell that Carole liked the idea of having an adventure to relate, but she hung back a bit.

"What if we get caught?" she worried.

"We won't," I assured her. "We'll do what Graham does. Move very carefully, make ourselves invisible and melt into the shadows. Plenty of them to melt into in that garden, after all."

"You know, that'll be why she lets it grow so wild," Carole realised; "to hide all the herbs."

"Come on, then!"

★ ★ ★

Now we are almost there we've slowed down a little. As before, we stoop by the hedges and the wall so we can't be seen. It's still easy to tell which is the right garden but I don't know yet how we'll get through the brambles.

"There's no fence between here and next door," I notice. "Only a low wall and bushes. We could sneak in from this side."

"But we'd be trespassing in two gardens, then," Carole points out. She's right, though it's a shame to turn back now with nothing to report. I stare through the gathering dusk towards the houses.

"Look, they've got their lights on and their curtains drawn. They'll never see anything. It'll only take us five minutes."

"All right, you go first," agrees Carole.

Giggling nervously, we haul ourselves up onto next door's wall, creep in and push through the bushes. I can't believe we are doing this!

Now we are actually in the witch's garden. No

sign of her or the cat. No toad or crow, either, that we can see.

"Remember what we're looking for," whispers Carole. "I've got the book in my pocket so we'll be able to compare the picture with anything that looks like Nightshade." *If we can see it well enough*, I think.

We're doing quite well with the snooping, hiding behind bushes and crawling carefully to examine any suspicious-looking weeds. Graham would be proud of us. We've got about a quarter of the way up the garden. It's going to be much easier than I expected so we'll soon

Bang bang bang bang!

It's coming from an upstairs window. There's a shape there with a beckoning finger. It must be the witch herself! She's tricked us into thinking no-one was in.

Flee! Back into shadows, through scratchy bushes, a wild jump down to the path, a race to the gate and faster, ever faster, down the hill.

We're panting so much outside Carole's house we can hardly speak.

"We made it!" I grin at her as my breath comes back.

Carole is bending over, strangely. "I've got a terrible pain," she says in a small voice. "We shouldn't have done that. Do you know what?" and there are tears in her eyes.

"I've been cursed!"

Nicola's 1st Verse

It's quiet in the classroom. We are all sitting, heads down, trying to write a composition. It's supposed to start with the words, 'What I would like to do most of all'.

It's all right for Jenny. She loves writing and is always first off the mark. She hasn't stopped since. In fact, everyone seems busy except me. The only thing I'm busy with is picking off my pink nail varnish.

I'm still feeling left out and unhappy. It's all Jenny's fault. I saw her pretending to be me, prancing about with a silly bin on her head, showing off and getting all the glory for making the others laugh. Don't they know how cruel she is? It's true what Mummy says, "It's always the quiet ones you have to watch."

There's been a lot of whispering around them today, her and Carole and Amelia. One or two of the boys as well. They seem to be plotting something and I'd love to know what it is. They won't tell me, though. Just change the subject loudly when they think I'm listening.

Why am I always left out? I try my best to be nice to them. I always show them my new things but nobody shares anything with me. Ever. Or only once, this week actually, when Carole gave me one of her Jammie Dodgers. I already had two in my pocket but took it because it was kind of her.

Perhaps I could take her home and show her my collection of jewellery. Then she might be my friend. That's an idea.

I pick up my pencil and start writing under 'What I would like to do most of all'.

Colin's 6th Verse

Babysitting in the evening isn't too bad really because Mum always makes sure the youngest family members are tucked up in bed before she goes for her night out.

It must be a hard life for her since Dad had that terrible accident. She works as many hours as she can in the lightbulb factory and then has the cooking and cleaning at home, as well as looking after us lot. My other grandmother, Nan, as we call her, gives a hand now and then, and Grandad cleans out the fire grate most winter days, taking out the ashes, rolling newspaper firelighters and then covering them with sticks. The first of the older children home, usually me, puts a match to it and fetches coal from the cellar.

I was glad to see the fire laid when I got home today. The cold, wet weather seems to have returned with a vengeance even though it's supposed to be spring. We soon had a good warm blaze, and after tea Mum agreed to let me go round to Carole's for an hour. "Back by seven at the latest," she reminded me. Fine; she needs time to relax a bit.

I was the last person to arrive at the society HQ and surprisingly Nicola Potts was walking around outside, aimlessly, in the drizzle. When she saw me she quickened her step, walking past me with a muttered "Hiya." Were Mummy and Daddy aware, I wondered? Most suspicious!

I knocked three times and gave the password. Carole had called this meeting in order for members' reports to be given after the holiday. There had been no time to write coded messages, she apologised, so she had resorted to whispering in ears during school.

She had managed to procure a bottle half full of Tizer and a packet of biscuits, so the meeting was already starting with a feast. Then it was down to business.

"First on tonight's agenda," began Carole, "is something we mentioned but never actually got round to. We need to find two places where we can leave society messages… Somewhere at school and somewhere outside near our homes. We'll all have to look there regularly in case anyone's left a note. Can any members think of anywhere?"

"It isn't going to be easy to find anywhere at school," Amelia realised, "with separate cloakrooms for girls and boys."

"What about the hall?" asked Jenny. "We're all in there at some time of day."

"Yes, but we're always under observation there," I pointed out.

"It could be in the classroom itself," suggested Carole. "There's odd moments when Mr Nuttall is marking or has his back turned."

"We could look for somewhere low down," Graham added, "near t' milk crate where we all go or, better still, *under* t' milk crate. How about having a quick look for a note whenever we collect our milk? If there's one waiting we grab it and decipher it behind our desk lids, then put it back when we've read it. Screwed up, it'll look like litter."

"Good thinking!" admired Carole. "Let's do that. Don't forget to have your code-reading strip somewhere inside your desk. We'll have to keep any notes as short as possible to read them fast enough for all of us to find them.

"All in favour? Right, I don't think we need to worry about an outdoor note hiding place yet because we're at school every day again now. Item 2, holiday reports. Has anyone done any helping or had any adventures they'd like to share?"

Everybody began to clamour at once so Carole stopped us.

"Quiet!" she ordered. "Members will pass the Golden Reindeer round in a clockwise direction.

Be careful with it. Whoever has it on their knee can speak without being interrupted."

I must say this for Carole, she knows how to run a meeting. She picked up the reindeer and placed it on Amelia's lap.

"Can I tell everyone about our Witch Watch?" she asked.

"Just one moment," came the reply, while Carole unearthed a small booklet from beneath a pile of boxes. "You'll need this."

Amelia told the story with relish. She made the historical background and then the following investigation in the darkening garden suitably scary, enjoying the impact on her listeners.

Carole took back the reindeer as she came to an end. "And after I'd had the curse put on me I felt strange all night, even when the pain had worn off."

Nobody spoke for a moment while we took it all in. But I was sceptical. "How long is it since you've had a stitch?" I asked her.

"That was no stitch," she replied, thoroughly convinced of the fact.

"Conclusions?" I asked.

Carole still had the reindeer. "All evidence to date remains highly suspicious. We must continue to observe."

Next it was Jenny's turn to take our emblem.

"I'm sorry but I haven't got anything to report," she said. "I suppose I did help in the shop a bit, filling up the shelves with tins of cat and dog food, but that's nothing new. Oh, but there's just the caretaker. I was on my way across the hall with a message that day the inspector came... Do you remember? Mr Nuttall had asked me to take a message to Miss Ingham. I was sure the hall was empty. Then I had a funny feeling, turned round, and he was right behind me." Jenny shivered at the memory.

This echoed my own experience, and I said so.

Graham held the reindeer next and related his story of following his football into the basement, where he had seen, or believed he had seen, Mr Grimes coming out of the shadows.

We decided that we did not like or trust the caretaker. We had to keep him under observation, albeit at a safe distance.

The meeting concluded on that note and I made my way through damp, swirling mist that seemed full of strange, long-legged people.

I'm so glad to be here, toasting my toes on a warm hearth. I'll go and check in a minute and see if the little rogues are asleep, and then settle down again with that book.

Jenny's 5th Verse

It's dinner time, and as usual I collected Julie from the Infants before we rushed home. Rain again!

We are pushing and struggling to be first through the shop door so we can stamp on the mat to dry our feet, water splattering from our gaberdine macs.

"Hello, Bertie!" our hill mynah bird greets us from his cage by the counter.

"Hello, Bertie!" we both shout together as we race across to the kitchen. "What are you doing?"

"What are *you* doing?" he replies as he always does and adding in a strict voice, "Mind your own business!"

A customer laughs and Bertie joins in, finishing off with a bout of hoarse coughing.

I don't know how Mummy gets a chance to cook us a dinner every day but she always does, usually with a pudding as well. Today it's liver, onions and mashed potato, followed by semolina. She comes to join us as soon as she can and asks us what we've been doing at school.

"Painting," says Julie, which isn't surprising as she has a yellow streak on her nose.

"History," I say. "I did a lovely drawing of a castle, and do you know what? In July we're going on a trip to Clitheroe Castle!"

"Lucky thing!" complains Julie. "I want to go too."

"When you're in big school you'll be able to."

Mummy looks at our side of the table. "If you both finish with clean plates you can choose a colour for your pudding," she promises.

It works. We just about finish, then I choose blue and Julie points to red, which on the white pudding makes pink. You only need two tiny drops from a little bottle to make a swirly pattern, or a paler colour when it's all mixed in. Then we are allowed sugar sprinkled on top. It's gorgeous.

All this time the kittens are capering around the kitchen, tumbling over each other when they meet. Tina jumps onto my knee for a stroke, setting up a deep, throaty purr while she watches them.

I sit thinking while I can't do anything else. I'm still feeling guilty about what I did last week. I don't really know what made me want to imitate Nicola like that. I'll never forget how upset she looked. Why did she have to come back and see it all?

She hasn't spoken to me since and I've avoided her. Really, I should tell her I'm sorry, I know I should. It's very hard though. What can I do to be nice to her?

Amelia's 6th Verse

Too wet to be outside tonight, so no Witch Watch. I don't mind; it's getting rather boring anyway.

I went up there with Graham last night after reminding him that he's supposed to be our spy. Absolutely nothing doing; no sign of life at all. Not even the black cat. We didn't stay long because it was too cold and I certainly didn't want to risk being caught in the garden again. Graham can try looking for herbs when the weather warms up!

Of course, it is exciting to allow ourselves to believe in the possibility of magic. On the other hand, I'm sure Carole can convince herself of anything when it suits her. I'm with Colin, thinking it was a stitch she had when she thought she'd been cursed. We had certainly been running fast, and she does love a bit of drama.

Yet I can't *quite* dismiss the idea of the existence of a twentieth-century witch. Who knows? If there was evidence for witches over three hundred years ago why shouldn't there still be some around now? They wouldn't *all* have been caught and a few of them must have had descendants. They would have learnt to keep their abilities secret over the years so that they could survive.

These were my thoughts as I was sitting at the table with my family an hour ago. On early closing day there are always the four of us plus my two aunts, one uncle and my grandfather. On the menu is usually a roast with all the trimmings, followed by tinned fruit with evaporated milk or custard.

What makes it special is the conversation. I'm the youngest, of course, but on these occasions I'm treated as a young adult, allowed to listen and even to have an opinion.

One of my aunts is a lawyer, well-educated and well-informed. My sister would like to follow in her footsteps. Pops and Uncle Raymond will often argue the case against my aunt, just for devilment. It makes for some really interesting debates.

I considered bringing up the subject of modern witchcraft tonight but the topic of the Cold War, and whether it was escalating out of control, was in full swing. I didn't like to admit that I had no idea what the Cold War was, so I kept quiet and made a mental note to ask Pops about it while we washed up after the meal.

"Oh, Amelia," interrupted Mum as I was about

to ask later. "I don't suppose you've seen this. You might find it interesting."

She handed me the *Free Press*, open at a page with a picture of a well-known Valley fishing spot. In a close-up shot just beneath it was Graham.

I read the article with astonishment. Rarely do we hear of such dramatic events round here, and there was Graham right in the middle of it all! What an adventure, and why didn't he even mention it at the last meeting? What a strange boy he is!

Nicola's 2ⁿᵈ Verse

Have you ever had a day that began like a nightmare but ended more like a good dream? That's how mine was.

When I walked into school this morning I wished I'd been able to stay in bed. Every time I went into the cloakroom the same memory was waiting for me – Jenny making fun of me, and all the others laughing. It's been horrible.

Jenny and I have avoided each other since. Not a nice person, I thought. In fact, in the whole school, who *is* a nice person?

There's only Carole, but even she is in league with them all.

At playtime she surprised me. She came over, put her arm round me and asked if I was all right.

"Course I am," I said, and then, "Well, not really. Nobody is friends with me since Jenny's silly performance."

"Right, let's get this sorted out. Come here, Jenny. *Now!*"

Jenny saw the two of us together. I could tell she didn't really want to come across, but she had no choice.

Carole's expression was determined. "Tell Nicola you're sorry!"

"Sorry," she mumbled, not looking at me. Then she did look up, right into my eyes. "Honestly, I really *am* very sorry, Nicola," she said. "I should never have done that. It was a nasty, stupid thing to do and I'll never do it again. Do you forgive me?"

"All right, then." It was good to clear it all up. Two seconds later I saw my chance.

"If you both really want to be friends, will you let me know what you've all been doing these last few weeks?"

Each of them looked away, so I added, "I've felt so left out of everything," and I put on the about-to-cry face that always works with Mummy and Daddy.

It worked again. Carole was thinking hard. "Well, I can't really tell you because some of us are doing secret work in the community."

"What, like spying?" I asked.

"Well, sometimes, but usually more like helping people."

"Oh, can I join in? You might get more done with an extra person."

"I don't know… I *could* ask the committee," she said. "We'll have to vote on it."

This was impressive. I'd only seen a few children going to her house but it sounded like something as important as a gathering of the council in the Town Hall.

"Maybe Nicola could help us tonight," Jenny suggested, "with our watch on the old lady."

"I'm not going there again," said Carole, "but *you* could take her, Jenny."

"Oh, I'd like to look after an old lady," I said.

"Er, yes, we just make sure everything is all right up there," said Jenny. "We don't go into her house; just look over the wall to check."

We arranged to meet after tea. Strange to think I'd be doing something important with somebody I'd started to think was an enemy. She wasn't an enemy now, though, and everything was at last getting better for me.

So, after school, when I'd eaten, I asked Mummy if I could go to meet Jenny at the pet shop. She was pleased I'd cheered up and that I had a friend to visit.

Jenny had her little sister with her. We went to this place called 'Private', and Julie was hanging back a bit. Jenny told her not to worry and held her hand. Julie started to say something but Jenny shushed her. She said that we were only going straight to the other gate at the end of the path. As we walked along I looked into the gardens. They were bright with daffodils and tulips, all except for one. I could see someone in that garden, looking across at us.

"Oh, what's *he* doing here?" I asked.

Jenny's face took on a strange expression and she began to walk faster.

"That's it, we've finished," she said.

We hadn't seen any sign of an old lady. It's all rather odd, but I'm starting to get a few friends again and that makes me feel much better. I wonder if they'll let me help more often now?

Graham's 6th Verse

14,22,22,7/26,7/21,18,5,22/7,12,13,18,20,19,7

That's what the screwed-up piece of paper under t' milk crate had on it. I didn't see it till I put my bottle back, when I saw it sticking out a bit. Playtime were about to start so I 'ad to 'ang back a minute and pretend to be rooting around behind my desk lid while I were getting t' code cracked.

I wonder how many of t' others found it. Standing here now at t' HQ door, it looks like they all did. Carole's let me in before I can even give t' password. They seem to be waiting for me.

"Oh good, Graham," says Carole. "Come in; you're our guest of honour tonight." What does she mean?

It turns out they've got this week's paper and they've all been passing it round. They want me to tell 'em exactly what 'appened up at t' fishing lodge.

That's summat I don't really like thinking about but they're all wanting to know. As I'm talking, I'm finding it a bit easier than I expected. At least it's a story wi' a happy ending.

"Well, I wish we had a medal or a special badge to give you," Carole says. "If you hadn't run so fast that little boy might have died. But please accept this sticky bun instead. A round of applause, everybody!"

I feel a bit silly when they all clap, but it's a lovely, tasty sticky bun.

"Next item. We need a secret ballot to vote on something. This is how it works. There are two cardboard boxes here. As you see, one's marked 'Yes' and one 'No'. When you've decided how you want to vote you pick up one of these stones and put it in a box. I know that usually we vote with a show of hands but, this way, no-one else knows how you've voted. All right so far?

"Good. Because I'd like us to make a decision about Nicola Potts. She has no friends at all and she'd like to join the club. What do you think?"

"*Nicola Potts!* I thought this club was supposed to be secret and exclusive," says Colin.

"But one more member might be useful," argues Jenny.

"Depends who it is," says Amelia. "D'you really think we can trust Nicola not to spill the beans about what we do? You know how much she talks."

"I think she'd be so grateful to be a member that she *would* keep our secrets," Carole replies.

"Do you think she'd be useful, though?" Colin again.

"She's already been useful," says Jenny, "but we'll come to that in a minute."

Carole looks at me. "What do you think, Graham?"

There *is* summat I want to say. "Well, if we're going to 'ave another member, it should be a boy, not a girl. It'd even things up."

"Ready to vote, then, everyone? When you've decided, you can pick up a stone."

We turn our backs on the boxes while each person makes their choice. Then Carole brings 'em to the table and tips 'em out. Two stones in the 'Yes' box, three in the 'No'.

"It's a very close vote," Carole says. "Nicola isn't going to join us. But perhaps she could be an Associate Member."

"What the 'eck's that?" I want to know.

"She doesn't come to meetings and doesn't know anything about the secret side of things but she can help out when we need extra people."

"Mmmmm, all right, that could be a solution. Then maybe we could ask a few boys later to do the same," Colin suggests. All of us think this is a good idea.

"Now, on to Item Three," says Carole. "Jenny has a report."

Jenny picks up the reindeer, which t' rest of us have forgotten about today. "Last night I was on Witch Watch. Nicola was with me but I told her we were just keeping an eye on an old lady, not that we thought she might be a witch. Anyway, we were going past her house when someone came out. You'll never guess who it was!"

"Father Christmas?" joked Amelia.

"Even stranger," said Jenny. "It was the new caretaker! So we went straight past. He must have seen us. What do you think he could have been doing there?"

"Havin' a meeting like we're doing now," I think out loud.

"But why would those two be meeting? Unless…" She frowned. "Do you think, if she's a witch, he could be a wizard?"

We all go quiet now. Could be why he's so odd and can appear out o' nowhere. There could've been more of 'em inside t' house too. In fact, could witches and wizards be moving in on us? That's a thought.

Amelia's 7ᵗʰ Verse

This morning was very odd. Jenny and I went down to the basement as usual to make the teachers' drinks. The state of the kitchen was disgusting! It seemed that no-one had bothered to wash up since the day before, when *we'd* done it.

"It's time someone else did this job now. We've done our stint," I complained. "I'm going to remind Mr Nuttall this afternoon that the monitors should be changed."

While we were waiting for the milk to boil, Jenny washed the dirty pots and it was my turn to dry. The tea towel was nowhere to be seen; yet another thing to grumble about. There weren't many cupboards for it to hide in… It wasn't there and it wasn't over the toilet either.

Eventually I remembered about the door next to the kitchen that leads into the passage with the boiler room to the left and the staff room to the right. There would be plenty of clean tea towels in the teachers' cupboards, I thought.

The door was sticking so I gave it a push. Immediately I staggered backwards in alarm as a stream of buzzing air seemed to rush past. Behind me, in the kitchen, a black cloud of huge flies circled the ceiling and then descended onto every surface. Stray insects found our hair, clothes and faces, and others were dropping into the pan of hot milk.

Shouting and screaming, we took the stairs up into school two at a time. When we fell into the classroom it caused quite a consternation. I don't know how long it took Mr Nuttall to calm the pair of us down.

In the playground later, Carole had a theory about the cause of the incident. She convinced Jenny that the witch's curse was still following us and that after catching us in her garden and sending Carole a pain, it was my turn for something nasty.

Not sure I believe that, but I know this... I won't be eating Eccles cakes for a while. Too much like flies wrapped in pastry!

Colin's 7th Verse

A sunny Saturday at last, and I'm a little closer to my goal after helping Gran with her shopping again. I now have another sixpence to put with the rest in my secret hiding place. Perhaps with birthday, and later Christmas, money I'll eventually be able to afford a toy microscope that has enough magnification power to be useful.

I'm just helping Gran down from the bus, when the headline on a billboard outside the newsagent's shop claims my attention.

MISSING MAN BELIEVED MURDERED, SAY POLICE.

We don't often see headlines as gruesome as that in this valley! How very strange; there must be evidence of a murder without a body. It may be in a local or a Manchester paper. There's no chance of finding out; we can't stop to buy one because Grandma's homecoming cup of tea is drawing her along like a magnet.

The dastardly deed could have been done anywhere, I consider, as I'm hauling the heavy shopping bags up the steep hill, or brew, as we call it, towards the house. Just imagine, it could have taken place in the ruins of the disused mill below us, and the murderer could have escaped to the hills, running up this very road. He'd have been out of breath and in a state of high anxiety. We could even be treading in his footsteps right now. What a chilling thought!

I am scrutinising the road and the narrow path ahead for any small item that the criminal may unwittingly have dropped from a pocket as he'd hurried along, perhaps checking that he still had his wallet. Even a discarded cigarette packet might be covered in his fingerprints or could have picked up a thread from his jacket that could be a vital clue to his identity. What a shame I haven't got my microscope yet.

"Can you put the kettle on, Colin, while I unpack all these bags?" asks Gran, and here we are, walking into her house.

Down to earth with a bump, I reluctantly forget crime scenes. I fill the kettle and turn on the gas, which hisses and then pops as it catches fire from the match.

"Eee, I *say*! Just lewk at that window! It's filthy when t' sun shines on it!" Gran frowns.

I look, and it is.

"I'd clean it myself but I'm in my Sunday Best," she says, glancing down at her smartest image. "It's hard for me an' all. I have to get a chair and climb up on t' slopstone." (This is the sink.) "Doctor sez I shouldn't stand on cherrs at my age. I might 'ave a dizzy turn."

Hmmmmm! All right, I've got the message. Grandma disappears into the other room to show Great Grandad some item in one of her bags, so I search a cupboard for something suitable for cleaning windows.

I work hard and fast, standing on the 'slopstone', using plenty of water with detergent, then rinsing it, and finally screwing up old newspaper to rub away the smears. I'm quite proud of what I've done.

The kettle is whistling and in comes Gran to turn it off. I enjoy the anticipation in the silence as she admires my work.

"You know," she begins, "let me tell you something, young Colin. You'll never get a window really clean if you do it when the sun's shining on it."

Would you believe it? A comment like that after all those hints. I shake my head. There can't be anyone in the world quite like my Gran!

Carole's 6th Verse

Well, now we've had the Curse of Pain and the Curse of Flies. What will it be next? Everything comes in threes.

How fascinating it was to discover that the two people we've been watching actually know each other. What a coincidence... If it *is* only a coincidence. There has to be a link between those two. It evidently isn't age or work so I do think that Graham is right. They are meeting for a purpose. Suppose it *is* a society. There could be dozens of witches and wizards around that we've never noticed, all casting spells, planning dark deeds and putting curses on people. The thought makes me shudder.

I must have started our club just in time for us to make the discovery. All that magic didn't get totally stamped out all those years ago after all. It's still very much alive. It probably just went into hiding behind closed doors and nobody noticed. We might need to increase our society membership after all, to cope with the extra observation we'll have to do, but we'll have to stay well hidden. I wish everyone had voted for Nicola to be a full member, but never mind, I'm sure we can keep her busy.

Thinking of keeping people busy brings my attention back to Jimmy. I've had to look after him longer than usual today because our mother has had one of her migraine headaches. Jimmy refused to go to church. Not even bribes worked. It's a relief to me; he causes too much trouble and he's too young to sit still for long really.

He'll be starting at the Infants next September so he'll soon begin to grow up then. Not too much, I hope. He's not usually too bad to look after, as long as I set up something for him to do. This afternoon I found his small building bricks and the farm animals. We used the squares on the carpet for fields and built a barn, then I curled up here on the settee with my book.

I can hear him pretending to be each animal in turn, making it talk as he moves it to join the others. I'm not getting much reading done.

"Here you are, cows; eat your grass," he tells them. "This one's getting big. She's going to have a scarf." It must be a calf he means.

No, I don't want him to grow up yet. Wait till I tell Amelia that! She'll love it!

Jenny's 6th Verse

Julie and I had one of our favourite jobs to do after school. There's a chewing gum machine on each side of the shop door and they both need filling by hand. The metal fronts have to be unlocked first. When they've been taken off, you can see all the mechanism inside and watch how it works when you put a penny in where the slot would be. It's fun to put the packs of gum in the spaces at the top, then slide them down their tracks. We're always allowed a pack each when we've finished filling them.

We were in the middle of the job when Graham and his pal, Michael, came past. They stopped and stood around hopefully, asking if we needed any help. We told them we couldn't give any gum away, but it was the machines themselves that fascinated them, so we let them have plenty of goes with the coins.

"Have you any more snakes in yet?" asked Michael, after a while.

"Not here, but there'll be some at the Rawtenstall shop," I told him.

Graham was grinning at his friend. "He bought a grass snake last year," he told us. "Where do you think he kept it?"

"In a fish tank with a lid but no water?" Julie asked.

"No. The daft thing put it in a rabbit hutch. Then he were surprised when it were gone t' next morning."

Michael looked sheepish but he didn't seem to mind us all having a chuckle.

"We've just been having a walk up Private," said Graham, with a few meaningful winks at me. "All very quiet but somebody's been digging up loads of soil in one of the gardens." A double wink.

"Have you got something in your eye, Graham?" asked Julie. "Do you want Mummy to look at it for you?"

Neither my caring little sister nor Graham's good friend had the slightest idea what the two of us found so funny.

Nicola's 3rd Verse

This morning at playtime, Carole and I were sitting on a wall sucking gobstoppers and watching the others. School is still getting better for me. I've got loads of friends again, and told Carole so.

"Well, of course you have," she said, "as long as you keep bringing sweets and giving them out. But what happens when your mum stops giving you money?"

"She won't," I told her. "She gives me anything I want. Anyway, if she does stop I can always ask Daddy."

"But that's all wrong! What I mean is, sweets are lovely treats but you shouldn't rely on them to get yourself friends." Carole took out her gobstopper. "Oh look, it's gone pink now."

Mine was still blue. "Well, it works. Everyone thinks I'm kind."

"For a few minutes, they do. Or as long as it takes to eat the sweet."

I was puzzled. This needed thinking about. "Well, what else can I do? It's all right for the rest of you. You've got brothers and sisters. You know how to get on with people. I bet you've never known what it's like to be lonely and left out. Even my parents are much older than everyone else's. I haven't any cousins either. There's no-one anywhere *near* my age in my family."

"Oh!" said Carole. "Oh, I didn't realise. That must be awful. You poor thing! And all this time we girls have been wishing we could be in your shoes – your beautiful, shiny, brand-new shoes with the gorgeous dresses to go with them. Most of our parents could never afford to buy lovely clothes like yours."

I smiled, knowing this already.

"But you do show off quite a lot, you know," she added. "That's what people don't like."

These words hit me like a punch in the stomach. I'd never thought about this possibility before.

"I'll try to change," I said, eventually, but had to ask, "If I can't talk about my clothes, what should I talk about?"

"I don't know; I don't have to think much about what I say. Anything else would do really." Carole was puzzling, wanting to help. "Just try not to talk so often about yourself and what you've done. You could ask the others what *they* like doing or what they think about something. That gives *them* a turn to talk as well and it gives you a chance to listen to them. That's important."

Perhaps she's right. I could give it a try. It might just work.

Graham's 7th Verse

I managed to get t' message to everybody this afternoon. I hadn't decided to call a meeting till dinner time, and by then t' milk crate had gone. I told Colin in t' playground but telling t' girls 'd be a problem, I thought.

Then I came up with th' answer. Country dancing! An ideal time to pass on a quick message because during some o' t' tunes you get to dance with everybody. I allus choose Jenny to start with. She's light-footed, not like some girls who tread all over your toes.

Anyroad, I had time to say, "Golden Reindeer tonight, five o'clock. All right?" All three on 'em 'ad t' same face – eyebrows up, big grin and a quick glance sideways to see if anyone else 'ad 'eard.

I didn't say owt to Nicola. She's not a proper member and, besides, she's been acting very strange today. She kept leaning across th' aisle between t' desks. Did I want a sweet? Did I want to borrow a pencil? What did I think about t' sums this morning? All sorts o' silly stuff.

Well, here I am in t' clubhouse and there's nobbut me and Amelia yet. I used to think Amelia were reight posh and too clever by 'alf but she tells me that since we've been in t' club she's realised we're all clever at something. I like her now. She's quite mad at times and makes us all laugh. She's wanting to know why I've called a meeting but I'm making her wait till we're all together.

After a few minutes we're ready to start.

"Now then, Graham," begins Carole. "It sounds as though you've something to tell us."

"Aye." I launch straight into it. "I've been watching t' old woman's house regular, like. She's not been there much but there's summat going on in her garden. There's a whopping great patch where someone, or some*thing*, has been digging. Every time I go, it looks bigger. Not just topsoil either, from what I can see. It looks deeper. Do you think it could be owt to do wi' magic? Can you read your book again, Carole, see if it mentions owt like that?"

"I'll have a look," she says. "Has anyone got any ideas?"

"Maybe it's a gigantic outdoor cauldron for spells for the whole valley," Jenny imagines. "Is it round-shaped?"

"Not really. I think it's bigger 'n even that'd be."

"Let's have a break and a think," Carole suggests. "I've smuggled a big packet of crisps out of the kitchen."

We sit and crunch for a few minutes, quiet for once. Then Colin chimes in.

"If this was a situation in one of my crime novels, that disturbed earth would be a clue that a hole had been dug to bury a body," he says, looking at me. "You would have been aware of a strong odour of decomposition – that's the body rotting – and there would have been loads of flies there."

"Didn't notice any flies," I shake my head.

"Wait a *minute!*" Colin looks excited. "Let's consider something else. There was a newspaper board headline on Saturday. Apparently the police believe that a murder has been committed but they haven't found a body. Unfortunately, I didn't get to read about it. Did anyone else, or have you heard anything? No? Well there must be some kind of evidence that the police have found. Perhaps it's a used weapon or a scene awash with blood. Sorry, Carole, I'm only surmising, don't worry. But we know our creepy caretaker goes to the witch's house. If he's the person who's been digging, and the hole hasn't been covered yet, then perhaps it really *is* for a body. He'll wait till it's deep enough and bury the body under cover of darkness."

"So you think we got it wrong?" asks Amelia.

"He isn't a wizard, after all. Just a humble *murderer!*"

"But we don't really know that for sure," says Jenny. "Where's the body if it's not in the garden yet?"

"I don't know. Where would be a good place to hide it?" asks Colin. "Somewhere dark where nobody goes. You'd be able to tell by the smell of death. Remember ages ago when we sneaked into the doctor's house? We saw those wet footprints and thought then that they were big enough to be his. That house would make an ideal hiding place. We should go and look."

"P'r'aps we don't need to." This is me. "I think I know exactly where t' body is."

They are all staring at me. I need to know something first. "What's t' smell of death like? Is it so strong it makes you feel sick and does it make your eyes water? Yes? Well, listen. Last week I went in t' basement after my football. Remember me saying? I wasn't in long enough to see much… just a few big sacks around. I couldn't have stayed any longer than it took to get my ball anyroad. There was this terrible pong. I've never smelt a stench like it."

"So, Creeps really has committed murder!" Amelia seems to be relishing it. "It's all in bits in the sacks in there!"

"Oh no, oh no!" Jenny looks terrified. "I think you're right. My dad sells maggots for fishing. They're bred on rotting meat, and if you ever go

143

past the hatching factory on the hills before the road gets to Todmorden, you have to close your car windows. That's the smell of dead flesh, and there's nothing worse. Oh and guess what else! Once the maggots for sale in our shop had been left out of the fridge too long. When my dad opened the container, loads of horrible great flies flew out. Just like those we saw at school when we opened that door to the basement, Amelia!"

It feels like a dark shadow shoots up and grabs 'old of us all. This isn't just an adventure anymore. We're all freetened to deeath.

"We need to tell someone grown up about this," Carole realises.

"The teachers won't believe us," says Colin. "They'll say we're making it up."

"Our parents won't be happy about what we've been doing."

"*I* know!" I've remembered summat. "What about that reporter who came to my house? She gave me her number, but we 'aven't got a telephone."

"I have!" says Amelia. "Leave it to me. First, I'll see if I can discover anything about a murder in the recent papers, then I'll ring her and see if she knows anything about it herself, or if she can tell us what we should do. It's time I did my job. I *am* chief information officer, after all!"

Good for Amelia. I'll find t' number and tek it to her first thing in t' morning.

Chorus – School 4

A monkey came to my shop,
I asked him what he wanted.
A loaf, sir, a loaf, sir.
Where's your money?
In my pocket.
Where's your pocket?
I've not got it.
Please… go… out!

Joyful young voices are singing 'Summer Suns Are Glowing' on a suitably sunny morning. Mr Gastley strolls to the centre of the end of the hall, where he has the best view of all the children.

"It's true. The better weather has arrived, the birds are singing and we're all hoping it will be a good summer this year.

"But I'd like to give you all a word of warning. It's still many weeks until the long holiday begins. It is very important to make the most of your education and to continue to work hard, even if the weather gets hot.

"You won't always be at school. There are many

long years of work in the real world ahead of you. The kind of job you will have depends entirely on what you do now. Don't be one of those people who spends their life regretting that they wasted their time at school, people who are stuck in tedious, low-paid jobs. If you want to get ahead, *listen* to your teachers, *appreciate* your free education and, above all, *always do your best!* Thank you, Mrs Ormerod."

Amelia's 8th Verse

I still haven't had chance to do my Golden Reindeer task yet. After school today Diana was waiting for me, wanting me to try the bass part of a piano duet for the Sunday School concert. She said it will be a good opportunity for ensuring regular practice for us both if we can learn it. She can't fool me. I know she wants to impress the young man who's training to be a curate.

She's doing her homework now, so I'll have to be quick. I've already looked through the *Free Press* but haven't found anything at all. Now I'm in the workshop with issues from the last two weeks. Plenty of reports of weddings, sports and cookery demonstrations but nothing about murders.

Next job, then, is to try that reporter's number that Graham gave me, so back to the house! The coast is clear in the living room. Fingers crossed that the shop keeps my parents busy a few minutes longer.

"Good afternoon, *Valley Free Press*."

"Oh, hello. Could I speak to Miss Jean Whittaker, please?"

"Speaking; how may I be of assistance?"

"Well, I'm a friend of Graham Tattersall's. Do you remember the boy you interviewed about the fishing lodge accident two or three weeks ago?"

"I do indeed. Is this to do with the same subject?"

"No, no, but my friends and I have reason to suspect somebody of a crime. We'd like to know if you've heard anything about a possible murder in the Valley."

"Can you tell me your name, please…? And how old are you, Amelia…? Have you spoken to the police about this…? No…? Well, that is the first thing you should do if you are serious… Sorry, of course you are… You want to meet me? Where, at your home…? At school…? No, I see… Well, yes, I could go to that address, if you prefer… Oh, three knocks and 'Antelope' or 'Reindeer'. I won't be able to meet you till next Monday, I'm afraid, but do be sure to keep safe till then. Stay well clear of all this and make sure you and your friends are always together. Don't go anywhere on your own… No, I promise I won't tell anybody else. Goodbye, and take great care."

That's that sorted out, then!

Nicola's 4th Verse

Would you believe it?! People are still being nice to me even though I've stopped taking sweets to school.

Even Jenny asked me to play with her today. She said I could see her kittens. I'd never been in her shop because I've never had any pets. Mummy said I could go after tea and she would collect me when she'd finished some shopping. That meant I wouldn't have much time but it would be better than nothing.

The first thing I heard in the shop was a strange voice laughing, followed by a loud whistle, then a cough. In a large cage a heavy black bird with a bright orange beak was hopping from one perch to the other. It turned its head to see who had come in.

"That's Bertie, our hill mynah," said Jenny, leading the way through a bead curtain to a very strange kitchen. Most of one wall was covered in wooden shelves stacked with open boxes half-full

of tins of cat and dog food. The opposite wall had a cooker, a fireplace with a brass fender, and a sink in the corner. There was a small table, one large chair and three smaller ones. Kittens seemed to be everywhere. Julie picked one up, and I sat down with it. The soft, fluffy little bundle curled up on my knee and let me stroke it very gently.

On the table were two empty Easter Egg boxes, a pair of scissors and several magazines. Jenny and Julie had been cutting out 'families' of children from advertisements. The boxes were houses for each family to live in. Julie turned some of the paper dolls over to show me the names and ages that Jenny had helped her to write on the back of each.

"The oldest in my family is ten," she explained.

"That's Rowena, this one. All the others are in between and these two are the youngest. Pixie is a half and Benny is a quarter."

Jenny was leaning over the back of her chair towards a space on one of the shelves, reaching a castle she had started to make from a cardboard box. She had glued toilet roll middles on two corners and covered it all in brown paper, crayoned to make it look like stone. The paper was cut at the top in the shape of battlements. She wanted to know if I had any ideas for making a drawbridge that would work. I wondered why she'd gone to all that trouble. Why hadn't she just asked for a castle for her birthday? And where were all their real toys anyway? I wondered.

There were two closed doors on the opposite wall of the kitchen. Behind one there were stone steps leading down to the cellar, they said, where their mother did the washing and where the toilet was, next to the coal cellar. *Ugh, fancy having to go down there on your own at night!*

"Where's your bathroom?" I asked.

Jenny opened the cellar door and pointed to a shape that she said was a bath hanging from a wall. "That's it," she said. "It goes in front of the fire on bath nights."

Just imagine!

The second door opened with a latch that made three loud clacks, and I followed the sisters up twisting wooden stairs to their bedroom. A double bed took up nearly all the space. There was no room for anything else except a wall cupboard with bookshelves, and a tiny, shared wardrobe. *Where they keep all their clothes, I can't understand.*

Julie introduced me to the sleepers tucked up in the bed: Golden Teddy, Brown Teddy, Horsie, Jenny's doll Elizabeth and her doll, Cockaw. Well, that's what it sounded like!

We went through to the only other room. It wasn't very much bigger. Some furniture round the walls, a television and in the middle a settee that had to be unfolded into a bed at night for their parents. On Sundays and Tuesday and Saturday nights this was their living room.

So that was it; their house. Only one more place to show me, if I didn't want to go down to the cellar. Behind a door in their bedroom was another wooden staircase that took us to a dusty little attic. It was mainly used for storing things that wouldn't fit anywhere else. Under the sloping roof were two dolls' cots, and in front of them stretched a wide rectangle of artificial grass. They sometimes brought the dolls up here to have a picnic, they said.

We heard a shout from downstairs. Mrs Wilkinson told us that Mummy had arrived to take me home, so I had to leave.

On the way home I was thinking that I'd hate to

swap my house for theirs. *They hardly have anything nice; they must be so poor.*

The funny thing is, I can't wait to go again. Why, I don't know. It must be that warm, friendly feeling when they let me into their lives for a little while. Another feeling too; those sisters talked as though they could make or do anything in the world, even if it was all just in their heads!

Colin's 8th Verse

The situation now in connection with our secret society is rather a sinister one. I must confess to being worried about it.

If our suspicions are correct, we must tread extremely carefully. As yet, Amelia has been unable to unearth any reports of serious crime in the neighbourhood but this could be because the discovery is still too recent to be featured in the weekly paper. The headline I saw was probably for an evening edition and would have missed the previous week's deadline.

Amelia also told us about her request to meet the reporter. It may prove to be a little unnecessary and melodramatic but I'm sure we all feel easier now. Perhaps the time really has come for an adult perspective on events. It's just unfortunate that we have to wait a few more days before help arrives.

Meanwhile, Graham and I have doubled up

to continue the spying activities. Now that we're watching the caretaker, we've decided we are in need of daily football practice after school in the playground. I am completely useless at any sport, of course, but it provides good cover. Graham even says I'm improving a little!

Tonight it was later than usual when he called for me. We are on our way now, though we don't seriously expect Creeps to still be there. We're talking about the finer points of the game that I don't understand, and Graham is explaining the offside rule. It's beginning to make sense, and as we approach our destination we automatically lower our voices.

Strange how different the school building seems as dusk is falling and how much larger it appears to have grown. It even seems to be looking out at us malevolently through the glassy eyes of its windows. The phrase, DANGER, KEEP OUT, insinuates itself from nowhere into my mind.

Perhaps it is influencing both of us. Graham stops abruptly mid-sentence as we pass through the gateless entrance to the grounds. Silent and cautious, we walk around the side and down the slope towards the boys' yard. Hardly any light here. It's thick with shadows. There's a sense that we are intruding.

Just the effect of an old building on a young imagination, I reason. We must get over it.

Wait! Is that my eyesight or is a shadow really moving down there, quite close to where the boiler room door would be?

It takes the form of a tall figure wrestling with a bulky sack, emerging backwards. A dim light from the basement illuminates him as the sack breaks free of the doorway. It's Creeps, of course.

All his concentration is focused on dragging his burden, but how long will it be before he stops to take a rest?

Silently we take a single step backwards up the slope, then another. Aware that the slightest sound could alert him, so close now, it takes a stupendous amount of self-discipline not to turn and run. Especially when we are trying to blank out the dreadful knowledge of what may be in the sack.

Still treading softly, rolling toe to heel, I'm praying that Graham has a firm hold of his football.

Step by step, the slope stretches, made endless by this nightmare.

Now the struggle below is too much. Creeps has dropped his burden and is straightening, turning towards us...

We are out of his line of vision! Grateful beyond belief for the solid corner of the school wall, our single reaction is to turn and race out to the street, hurtling along the pavement towards the far end and the junction with the main road.

Graham darts behind a parked car, where we can

recover whilst still keeping an eye on the road. I'm holding my chest, hoping I'm not going to have an actual heart attack. It sounds and feels as though I am.

"He must be getting rid o' t' body," gasps my friend. "He'll 'ave a car waiting. He'll prob'ly come this way so he can get to t' street behind t' old lady's. I can't see him but he won't be far behind us. Let's dodge back behind t' cars till we're a bit nearer and can see better, in case he goes in t' other direction."

We listen intently, creeping across the long distances between the few cars.

Many different sounds float towards us as dusk deepens rapidly. I hear the swish of occasional traffic on the road, the slam of a door, a cat's warning. A window rattles and shudders as it is opened, the insistent persuasion of a television advertisement leaking into the air. Normal background noises that I don't usually notice. Strange how menacing they can sound in this darkening street, where neither of us has any business to be at this time.

An engine splutters into life and a small van, its lights off, is approaching. Instinctively we duck down, peering over a car bonnet. As we anticipated, the driver is Creeps.

The same thoughts occur to both of us as we gaze after him. Will the hole in the old lady's garden be filled in by morning, covering the dreaded contents of the heavy sack? He's not going to get away with it; we'll make sure of that. We know now, though, that we need to enlist professional help. Our part in it is almost over.

Funny how, in real life, crime loses its fascination when you're getting close to danger. All I want to do now is get straight home and listen to my brothers and sisters arguing. The louder the better. Best of all will be to enjoy the scolding I'll get from my mother for being so late home! Who knows, I might even tell her what I've been doing.

Carole's 7th Verse

I've called an emergency meeting of The Golden Reindeer for playtime this morning. Right here, in the open! It's the only thing to do.

Earlier, as I was walking to school, I noticed Colin waiting by the wall for me. He told me everything that had happened last night. Events seem to be moving so fast, in a direction that we should no longer have anything to do with, I thought. So now we are gathering in the gap between the girls' and the boys' playgrounds. Usually this gap is almost invisible; we all know it's there but always act as though it is a continuation of the solid wall. Nobody crosses it; why would we?

Nicola is walking past, pretending not to see us. I reach out and grab her, pulling her into the midst of our huddle.

"Come on, we need every single member of The Golden Reindeer," I tell her. "We are all in serious danger!"

Nobody objects. I watch Nicola's eyes grow wider by the second as I quickly explain our recent discoveries. Colin and Graham bring the girls up to date with last night's news. Morning play is only short, so we all know that time is precious; decisions have to be made fast.

"How many people think our caretaker is a murderer?" I ask.

"The evidence is almost indisputable," asserts Colin, as six hands are slowly raised.

"Do we need to tell somebody *now*?" My legs are actually shaking, I'm so scared. I see from the expressions of the others that I'm not alone.

"But why not wait till the reporter meets us," suggests Amelia. "If *she* thinks we have a case, we'll tell the police, but if we've got it wrong, nobody else needs to know and we won't be laughed at."

"No, we're not seeing her till after the weekend," Colin says. "It's too long to wait."

"He's right," agrees Nicola. "You can't risk waiting another day."

"That's true; we shouldn't be keeping a secret as dangerous as this," adds Jenny. "We're not old enough."

"All right, quickly!" I say. "Everyone who thinks we should tell a grown-up today, put your hand up now!"

Every single one of them puts their hand straight up.

"I've got both hands up!" grins Graham.

I'm so glad, I could hug them. But as we're trying to decide who to tell, the bell is rung.

"My Mum!" or "My Dad!" they're all shouting as we break up to run across to our separate lines.

Before the prefects get each of us to shut up I shout at the top of my voice, *"Tell them all!"*

Jenny's 7ᵗʰ Verse

I am just so, so glad we've decided to tell people about the last few weeks! When The Golden Reindeer started it was great fun. I looked forward to every meeting with excitement. I never knew quite what to expect but I enjoyed having a useful part in it. Each of us felt that our opinions were valuable, and all our ideas were listened to.

After a month or so, though, it began to change. Small things at first but then it felt as though we had all been gathered up and rushed along into something that was getting more and more complicated and ugly.

I wonder if it was anything like this for the Pendle Witches all those years ago. I read about them in Carole's booklet. Most were ordinary, simple folk living in a difficult time. They didn't have much control over their own lives and it probably flattered them to be thought of as being a bit special. Then everything became more complicated. They were blamed for anything that went wrong, and their neighbours turned against them through fear and suspicion.

We were a bit like that with the old woman. We wanted excitement, and just a few little things led us to believe she was a witch. We never tried to visit her properly or offer to help her with her garden.

Perhaps we've got it wrong again with the caretaker. He might not be a wizard or even a murderer. But Colin said what we all thought: it's possible that he could be, because of everything we've seen and experienced that could well be proof. I hate to think that there may really be a body involved and, even worse, that it was here in the basement!

We do need adults now to help us sort it all out. So it's going to be Mummy first, as soon as I get home, and Daddy later.

"Jenny!" Mr Nuttall's voice makes me jump. "Are you daydreaming again? I know it's been a long day but would it be too much to ask you for some concentration for the remaining five minutes of it?"

Whoops, better finish this! Whoever invented stupid arithmetic? What do I care how long it takes to fill a leaking bath? Get a plumber to fix it! How many of us toiling here in this room have a real bath, anyway?

★ ★ ★

Time to go home at last. Our class is last out because we needed a little reminder about working hard, Mr Nuttall said. In the cloakroom I exchange cheerful smiles, waves and winks with Amelia, Carole and Nicola. We share a feeling of great relief now the burden of our secret knowledge is about to be shed. This weekend will be even more enjoyable than usual. It's good to have Nicola with us properly, I think.

Oh dear, last to leave again! One of my sandals has been kicked right to the other end, under the bench. It's quite a stretch to reach it, too.

"Hello, Jennifer."

It's him*! He can talk.* He's standing near the door to the basement steps… *The basement…* How does he know my name?

He's coming nearer. "You're not frightened of me, are you, Jennifer? You looked really scared just then."

There's no-one else here.

He comes closer still.

I can't hear anybody in the hall. The teachers don't stay long after us, I don't think. They might even leave at the same time on a Friday.

"I'm not going to hurt you, you know."

Help, help! Nobody knows I'm still here. The Reindeer Club members aren't supposed to be alone. That was the plan.

I could run into the hall; I could run into a classroom – but there are no locks on the doors.

I'd be trapped. The windows are too far above the ground to climb through. There's no exit from the hall. He's between me and the door out of school. The basement door is still open but he's blocking that too. *Don't* think *about the basement.*

"What's the matter?"

Could I get through the hall to the boys' cloakroom and to that exit fast enough or might he have locked it already?

"Honestly, I don't bite." He sits down on the bench opposite where I'm standing, frozen. Have I room to dodge around him and run to the boys' cloakroom anyway now or will a long leg shoot out to send me sprawling?

Stay calm. Think of Julie waiting for me in the Infants next door.

"Haven't I seen you up the hill on the path with the gate that says 'Private'?" he asks. So he *had* seen us.

"Oh, you're surprised, arc you? I've seen you with your friends."

What can I do? What can I do?

There is movement at the door to the basement steps as someone else appears. *Two of them*, I panic. Now I'm really trapped.

Wait a second, he looks completely different without his usual boiler suit, but... yes, it's...

"Fred!" I shout, and I've never been as pleased to see him. There he is, as large as life, walking closer to sit next to his replacement.

"Oh, that's done it!" says Creeps. I look at him and he is smiling. Creeps! I didn't know he *could*!

"You've managed to do the trick. I've been trying to talk to her for five minutes but she won't answer."

"I told you, Alan," says Fred. "Children are only t' same as adults. They don't like to be ignored but they don't like you to talk down to 'em. You must 'ave been doing summat wrong. Pretend she's seven foot tall and looking down on you."

A giggle escapes me but I'm completely baffled. The danger is going, though, fast.

"'Ere, what've you been doing while I've been away, then?" Fred asks me.

"Oh, playing at witches and wizards," I hear myself babble crazily, "and other things." I catch my breath and struggle to get back to normality. "Did you see Graham in the paper?"

"I did, that! Little lad were nearly a goner by t' sound."

"He was. Are you in your new bungalow now, Fred? What's it like?"

"Grand. Buses to t' sands are every ten minutes so we're allus there when it's fine. Patch loves it. He runs for miles on t' beach. Likes a paddle too if we get near enough. Anyroad, how's Alan doing? He told me he were a bit nervous of tekkin' t' job at first. Not used to children, you see."

What? Creeps afraid of us? This is unthinkable!

Now he is smiling quite naturally. I'm fascinated to see how much it changes him.

"Well, I've never had chance to get used to 'em," he says. "You're all a bit like aliens to me and none of you talk to me either. *You* wouldn't talk to me just now! I had to get a new job when me and my old mum came to live here, and this were t' first 'un I could find."

"Oh, so the w… the old lady is your mother?"

"You've noticed her? She said she'd seen a few children around. She knocked on t' window once, thinking they might like a scone fresh from t' oven, but they ran off. Must've thought she were going to tell 'em off. She thinks that wild garden might've been their place to play, it's so long since anyone lived there. It were cheaper to buy for that reason but it needs a lot of work done on it, inside as well as out. I'll get it done eventually. I'm digging a pond just now, a big 'un. If any of you and your pals'd like to give us a hand, my mother's always got a bit of baking ready for a job well done. Spread the word!"

"Ohhhhhhhhh!" is all I can say as things click into place.

"Well, don't forget. We'd better get these sacks off to your place now, Fred. He gave me a right job an' all," he says, laughing at Fred.

"I did," admits Fred, "but not on purpose. When we moved I couldn't get everything in t' removal van."

I remember him talking about it before he left, and say so.

"Alan had t' bright idea of storing t' rest in t' boiler room, see. So he helped me take it all down there."

"What I *didn't* know was what I were letting myself in for." Alan shakes his head. "You should've smelled the awful stench coming from one o' t' bags after a while. A few days later t' place were full o' bluebottles."

"We saw them," I gasp, "when we were making drinks for the teachers. Me and Amelia. They came right into the kitchen! Scared us to death!"

"Well, I weren't to know Patch had taken his new bones and dropped 'em both in one o' t' sacks ready for tekking to t' new house, were I?" asks Fred. "He must've wondered why they'd never turned up. Full o' meat, they were, an' all."

"I suffered that smell every time I went down there," laughs Alan.

"I didn't have time to sniff out the problem till last night, when I were passing and decided to solve it once and for all. They're buried in t' flower bed now. Don't tell your headmaster!"

The pair of them chuckle like naughty schoolboys, and I join in. Once started, I can't stop and the three of us are helpless, thinking about what Mr Gastley would say.

It's such a relief to laugh, and even funnier for

168

me because they don't know the rest of it. "We thought you were a wizard!" I manage between gurgles.

"A *what*?" asks Alan in complete amazement, and we're all off again. "Oh, that's priceless! Now I know I'm going to like this job, after all."

I can't tell him yet what else we thought he was. That'll be for when we get to know him better. At this rate, it may not take too long.

"Come on, Fred. Time we were going," says Alan; "and thanks for talking to me at last, Jenny. Don't stop, will you?"

"I won't," I promise, gathering my belongings happily. "I'll introduce you to all my friends on Monday. And if you know anything about football, you're *in*!"

"I might just take you up on that," he says. "Girls as well as boys, eh?"

Graham's 8th Verse

Me and Colin have been sitting on t' wall since school finished, talking about how scary it were last night when we saw Creeps wi' t' sack. We know we'll 'ave to spill t' beans now, but there's two of us 'ere. Should we go up one last time, see if t' 'oyle in t' witch's garden's all filled in and planted as if that's what were intended all t' time? It could be full o' roses now. Nobody'd know what's underneath.

Hush, someone's coming out o' school behind us. They're making plenty o' noise, luckily, else they'd've heard us.

I nearly fall off t' wall! It's Creeps, with Fred and Jenny. All laughing and chattering, pally like. *She's* changed her tune.

"Now, then, you two! How's tricks?" Our old chum's beaming at us.

"Fred!" we both shout. "Are you coming back?"

"Not for long, but I'll be back for a proper visit

170

as soon as I can drag Mrs H away from t' seaside. Then I'll want to see 'ow your football's coming on. Ask *him* to keep you going till then!" He gives Creeps a nudge as they climb into a van. I'm sure it's t' same van we saw last night. There's summat different about Creeps, though. Jenny sits down wi' us while we wave to Fred.

"How strange," says Colin. "He actually looks human, for once."

"He *is* human," Jenny replies, "and guess what? He isn't a murderer."

We stare at her. She's convinced.

"Come on," she says. "I've got Julie to pick up. Then we're going to collect all the others. I'm taking you for a picnic and I'll tell you all about it. Won't take long but everyone needs to hear this together."

Too flummoxed to argue, brains bashed to bits, we trail behind her, collect Julie, then go across to Carole's.

"It's like the old Chicken Licken story," Jenny chortles. "We're collecting Turkey Lurkey, Goosey Loosey, Ducky Daddles and all the rest. But we're telling them that the sky *isn't* falling."

"And is there a Foxy Loxy waiting in his wicked den?" asks Colin.

"Oh no, not anymore. Just wait and see!"

She won't say another word however much we try.

★ ★ ★

Twenty minutes later every club member plus Nicola, Julie and even little Jimmy are climbing rickety wooden stairs up to t' pet shop attic. Luckily, Mrs Wilkinson didn't make a fuss when all t' lot of us crowded into t' shop. She even found some sliced bread and cream cheese so we could make our own butties.

Jimmy can't wait. He started eating his bread climbing t' staircase even afore we all sat down on this patch of funny grass. (Grass in an *attic?*)

So now Jenny's telling us all we need to know and chewing at t' same time. A rum tale it is, too; plenty o' scary bits.

Carole's 8th Verse

What a story! I'm glad it didn't happen to me; I'd have *died!* I never thought when I started this club that we'd end up in an adventure like this.

What I really find impossible to imagine is Creeps smiling and laughing, but it must be true. Colin and Graham said it transformed him! I suppose we'll have to find a new nickname for him now. Fancy him being human, after all! They do say truth is stranger than fiction.

Sounds like we'll be able to carry on with one aim of the club this summer: helping people. We can regularly visit the old lady to help with that tangled garden. Maybe we'll have to go every day if her baking is as good as it sounds!

Funny how quickly we had all jumped to quite ridiculous conclusions. Amelia will have to cancel the meeting with the reporter. Good job none of us had time to tell our mums and dads. They'd never let us play out together again!

"Well, Detective Sergeant Ingham, it looks like you've got it wrong this time," I tease Colin.

"And a good thing too!" he says.

We all agree, while Jenny opens a bottle of fizzy lemonade. "Let's drink to that," she says. Amelia, Julie and Nicola sort out the mugs, and Graham pours.

"Can I have some more?" begs Jimmy, holding out his empty glass. The rest of us haven't even started. Trust him!

Final Notes

The intense blue of a Mediterranean sky has wandered off course to settle hundreds of miles away, bringing surprise and delight to Northern England. The sun of childhood memories finds colours from an artist's palette in all it warms. The vibrant and varied greens of the sycamore leaves on Thornfield Avenue send dancing shadows onto the stone of the school below, itself aglow with almost-forgotten ochres.

Patches of kaleidoscopic colour spilling out of the old building resolve into a long gaggle of children following their headmaster to form a wriggling line next to a gleaming yellow coach.

Excited chatter builds up. Lunch bags are compared and the contents discussed, some arrangements made to swap. Mr Nuttall strolls by, counting his charges yet again.

"I like your new sandals," says Nicola to Amelia. "Where did you get them from?"

"Not Manchester," grins Amelia. "Just from Eva's shoe shop up the road."

"Colin," says Graham, "I want to ask you what you'd think about my pal, Michael, joining us in t' club. He doesn't go to our school but he doesn't live far away. We can talk about it on t' coach."

"And about my new microscope too," says Colin. "I'm hoping to buy it at the weekend."

"*Aaaaaaaaaa!*" a piercing scream from Nicola. "My dress! It's got caught in something!"

Part of the lace trim of her beautiful new lilac dress is trailing along the pavement towards Mrs Barker's umbrella, propped against the wall.

Nicola's face is downcast, her lower lip starting to tremble.

Conversation has stopped.

She's going to start skriking, thinks Graham.

A new determination replaces Nicola's expression. She gathers what is left of the trim, rips it off smartly and throws it to the ground. Next to her, Carole, Amelia and Jenny stare, dumbstruck. Then Jenny crushes her in a warm hug. "Sit next to me!" she beams.

"All here now," Mr Nuttall informs the Head.

"Ready, boys and girls?" asks Mr Gastley. "You'll be getting on the coach in a minute and sitting with your partners. Remember what I told you about being on your best behaviour and setting an excellent example for your school. I must say that if the last few weeks have been anything to go by, I'll be very happy indeed. I'm proud of the way you have knuckled down to hard work, even on hot days like today. Some of you haven't found everything easy but you have all done your best and excelled yourselves.

"As a reward, I've decided to treat each of you to an ice cream when we arrive in Clitheroe. Well done, all!"

A stunned silence, then a call for "Three cheers for Mr Gastley!" probably from Colin.

As the cheers fade the first children board the coach while those at the far end turn and wave to Mr Grimes, who has come to watch them leave.

Relaxing into the unaccustomed luxury of comfortable, well-upholstered seats, the occupants of the coach watch reflections chase along its wide windows as it pulls away, glides to the end of the road and turns right.

Here, two clear voices start the singing, which is almost immediately swelled by all. The songs are sung as streets are left behind, alongside the Whitewell as it flows towards them from its source above. They are sung below the fishing lodge of Graham's adventure, through the village of Lumb where Jenny used to live, and Water, where she attended the tiny school, then past the end of Dean Lane, where Colin's dad used to take him for walks before he had the accident.

The singing lifts the coach ever higher up the winding road to the moors, where skylarks provide a musical accompaniment to the melody. The passengers are carried forward into a day bright with hope and with the promise of new memories yet to be made.

★ ★ ★

Alone in the boiler room, Alan Grimes smiles into his mug of tea.

> *Ickle Ockle Chocolate Bockle*
> *Ickle Ockle OUT!*